I0545687

Hidden Truths

Silent Witness

M.A. Bridge

CONTENTS

Ch 1

Seniors fight tooth and nail to survive to graduation. By all accounts, I shouldn't have made it. But I did. And while so many people kept me tethered, some days death felt like a better option than living. As I reflect back on my senior year—what I learned, what I lost—I'm grateful to be here. And yet, the ceaseless pit that made its home in my stomach years ago continues to churn.

It was midday in the beginning of August. The halls of my highschool buzzed with the anticipation of fellow seniors. I had just emerged from a crowd of students heading towards the cafeteria when I lost my footing, landing flat on my face and scattering my books and papers. I could feel my face flush and turned my head away from onlookers. While most of the crowd stood by and laughed, one person emerged to help me up.

"Hey, are you okay? That was a pretty nasty spill you just took," said a boy's voice.

As I got up, I felt his arm wrap around my side to give me leverage. I turned to see who the mysterious helper was and came face to face with the most amazing blue eyes — a bright memory flashed of the first time I saw the ocean. And even though my body was being lifted, it felt as though my stomach stayed where it was.

"Yeah, I'm great. Thank you for your help," I said as he helped me grab all my stuff. As soon as I had all my belongings in hand, I quickly walked to my finance class.

Mrs. Richards started her lecture, and my mind drifted off. Who was that boy? Why had I never seen him before? As questions ran through my head, the teacher called my name, shocking me back to reality.

"Olivia? Do you know the answer, or should I call on someone else?"

I quickly glanced at the board, doing the math in my head, and answered, "It's three thousand, four hundred and thirty-two dollars and forty-six cents." Mrs. Richards, shocked, nodded her head in approval. Class went on for another twenty minutes, and I dashed out as soon as the final bell rang.

Being a senior had its advantages. I only had four classes, and it allowed me to leave early enough to avoid any more humiliation regarding my spill. I decided to walk home instead of taking the half-day bus. I put my headphones on and walked to the beat of the music. It wasn't until I was about halfway home that I felt a presence following me. Quickly, I turned around to find the boy who had rescued me earlier that morning following closely behind. I slowly lowered my headphones around my neck and waited for an explanation.

My expression must have given away what I was feeling because he suddenly stopped to explain himself. With his hands in the air, he said, "I swear I'm not following you."

Thinking he might live nearby, I asked, "Do you live near

here?"

"Yes, actually. I live on 57th avenue and Baker. What about you?"

"Um. Uh," I stuttered. This boy inspired a million questions, but two in particular stuck out: who was he and why did he seem so familiar?

"I think I live on the same street."

"No way? How come I have never seen you around here before?" He asked the same question that had been on my mind earlier that day.

"I was just wondering the same thing. I've lived here most of my life, so I would think that seeing you would have been inevitable."

"Guess the world has a funny way of working things. Oh well, we've met now, so that's what matters," he said with a gleam in his eye.

He finally introduced himself to me. His name was Nathan Holtz, and he had played varsity for multiple sports for my school, including football, soccer, and golf. Even though I kept up with the Hillsboro High sports, I guess I was never really interested in the players. We kept up a conversation until we got to his house, which was closer than mine. He asked me how far my house was, and I said it wasn't too far, just a few more houses down. Nathan insisted on walking me the rest of the way, and since he was so persistent, I obliged.

"So, you're a senior, right? Are you planning on playing sports in college?" I inquired, curious to know more about this mystery man.

"I'd love to play if I make a team, but I'm just hoping to get into one of my dream colleges whether or not I get to play," he replied.

"Well, for what it's worth, I hope you're able to have both," I said. I knew that dream all too well — sacrificing half of yourself to pursue the other is an incredibly difficult decision for anyone.

Before I knew it, I was on the steps of my front porch saying goodbye to him. I suddenly felt a nervousness in the pit of my stomach, which I found to be odd at this moment since I felt comfortable with Nathan.

"Oh wait! I forgot to give you something," he said as he handed me a folded piece of paper, looking down towards his feet as the apples of his cheeks started to turn red. He quickly turned and left, and my eyes followed him as he walked away. As he did, I could have sworn that he looked back. I turned back to my door, having to focus a little more than usual on putting the key in the lock. Even when I was inside my bedroom, I couldn't shake the feelings of excitement and nervousness that had overcome me. Instead of doing my homework as I had planned, I laid down on my bed to think. Within minutes, I was asleep, drifting into my own world.

There was a knock on my bedroom door, and I jolted awake. My mom popped her head in and saw that I had been lying on my bed.

"Are you okay, honey?" she asked with visible concern.

"Oh yeah," I responded. "I guess I fell asleep. What's up?"

She looked me over one more time before she responded.

"You were just so quiet, I thought I would come check on you. Just make sure you do your homework, please." And with an apprehensive look, she closed my door and headed downstairs.

I started my homework, barely able to focus on the math in front of me. The only thing I could think about was Nathan and what he had done for me. Then I remembered the note he handed to me before he left. I looked through the piles of papers on my bed until I found the folded one he had given me. I opened it slowly, nervous about the possible contents. Inside it read,

"In case you ever trip again, here's my number."

Instantly, I could feel a wide grin creep across my reddening face. "Wow, this boy might actually like me," I said to myself (under my breath, of course).

The next day at school, I was hoping to see Nathan in the halls. Throughout the morning there was no sign of him. I decided to stay during lunch so I could eat with some of my friends. We sat down in our usual place on the grass and started catching up since we hadn't had the chance for a couple of weeks. And, just as I had expected, they had all heard about my incident the day before.

"What happened? I heard you broke your nose when you fell," Lissa said without hesitation.

I looked at her, and though I wondered where that rumor came from, I replied in my most serious voice. "Yup. Doesn't the broken nose suit my face well?" I made a grand gesture towards my face. Unable to withstand the urge, I started to giggle. They all began cracking up as I continued to say, "I obviously didn't break my nose, but I did meet a cute new boy. He even lives near me."

Almost as though they had been practicing, a simultaneous "Oooohhhh??" broke out amongst my friends. "What's his name?" they asked, nearly in unison.

I made eye contact with Emma, my best friend, who already knew more than the rest of the group would ever know.

"His name is Nathan," I replied, feeling a grin creeping back onto my face, making me feel like the Cheshire cat.

"What about me?" a familiar voice asked from behind me, causing me to jump.

"Oh, uh, um, I was just explaining how you helped me yesterday when I fell," I stuttered, feeling my face redden as I turned towards him.

"Oh yeah? Did you tell them how I swept you off your feet, too?" He winked, which just caused me to blush harder. Little did he know, he really had done that. But I laughed it off, doing my best not to show how much his presence affected me.

We all spent the lunch period getting to know each other, and as soon as the first bell rang, I started the walk to my house. Because it was a habit, I put my headphones on and started blasting my favorite playlist that consisted mostly of Linkin Park and Bring Me The Horizon. I wasn't even 50 feet away from the edge school when I felt a hand on my shoulder. I jumped, not used to being approached on my walks home. I turned to see Nathan standing next to me, with a big smirk on his face.

As I pulled off my headphones, he said, "Sorry, I should probably stop doing that, huh?"

I looked at him and smiled, but I also nodded in agreement. We walked in silence for a few minutes, both of us thinking about what we had to do when we got home.

Nathan was the first to speak. "By the way, thank you for letting me eat lunch with your group. I wasn't planning on staying, but I'm glad that you all were so inviting."

"Of course, you're more than welcome to have lunch with us whenever you'd like. My friends seemed to like you, so it shouldn't be a problem," I said, smiling.

"Well, I really appreciate it. What do you have to do tonight?" he asked. "Just homework?"

"Actually, I have no homework tonight. But I did want to go see a movie, especially since we have tomorrow off."

Nathan's expression told me that he had no clue we had the next day off from school. And his response matched my assumption. "What? Since when do we not have school tomorrow?" He asked, with an obvious look of concern. He then continued by asking, "Are you messing with me?"

Normally I wouldn't have been able to suppress my laughter, but it was apparent by his seriousness that I should make an attempt. I responded, "No, of course not. Honestly, there's no school tomorrow because of some special in-service thing for teachers. I think it's basically a day for them to catch up on all the stuff they are behind on. It's quite nice actually. Helps the teachers get organized, and usually, that helps their moods too!" I soon realized that I sounded like a complete nerd and hoped that he would not point it out.

He formed an expression on his face that I could not read. "Are you okay, Nathan?"

He quickly came out of his daze and replied, "Oh yeah! I'm fine. Mind if I tag along tonight? I can even pay for your ticket?"

"It would be my pleasure," I said with a smile, trying to put him (and myself) at ease. "But I'm not going to let you pay for my ticket."

"Hmmm. Well, that's too bad! Because I'm going to anyway!" Nathan exclaimed.

As we reached my house, I puffed a breath of relief that contrasted the red in my cheeks. Once again, I fumbled with my keys but managed to quickly put the correct one into the lock. Before I could close the door, I heard Nathan's voice say he would pick me up at seven. The door closed behind me, and I slunk down to the floor, feeling as though my legs were jello. Once the numbness went away, I watched my favorite show, *Modern Family*, overthinking the impending situation and using the show as a distraction. After the episode was over, I ran up to my room in hopes of preparing the perfect outfit for that night. The only thing I could think to myself was how I wanted this date to be perfect. I could feel a wave of anxiety start to wash over me, but I forced myself to ignore it as I tried to prepare myself for the night.

As I rummaged around my closet for the perfect outfit, I heard a knock.

"Yes?"

"Can I come in?" a timid voice asked from the other side of the door.

"Of course." Hearing my approval, my little brother walked in holding a notebook in one hand, and his math book in the other.

"I need your help on my math assignment," he said with a

frown across his face.

"Okay. What are you working on?" I asked with a calm and reassuring tone to put him at ease. I sat down on the bed, motioning for him to sit next to me so I could help.

"Geometry," he said as his shoulders dropped. "I hate this class. I can never seem to figure it out."

"It's okay, I had problems with this class too until I got a tutor who could teach me the way I understood it best. We'll figure it out." And with that, Will and I spend the next four and a half hours working on practice problems and his homework. I managed to find ways to explain each type of problem in a way he understood and could reproduce with his homework.

I was so invested in trying to find better ways to teach my brother that I didn't realize how much time had passed. It was now 6:40, and I only had 20 minutes to pick out an outfit and get ready. As I stared at my closet, I wondered why I cared so much about what I was wearing since I normally just cared about being comfortable. With that thought in mind, I grabbed a pair of skinny jeans, high tops, and a simple tank top from the closet and put them on. I walked into the bathroom, pulled the hair-tie out of my hair, put a little mascara on my eyelashes, and went downstairs.

Right as my foot touched the bottom step, I heard the doorbell ring. As I approached the door, my nerves overcame me. My hand was shaking as I opened the door to a smiling Nathan with flowers in hand.

"Hi Nathan! Who are those for?" I asked, confused.

"Oh, you know, my secret girlfriend next door. Figured I'd drop them off before we went to the movies," Nathan said jokingly. "Just kidding! They're for you of course."

And there was that smile again.

I thanked him, shyly taking the flowers from his hands. I invited him in, heading towards the kitchen where I could find a vase. As I entered the kitchen's threshold, I could see my mom standing by the kitchen island.

"Oh, those are pretty? Who are those from?" my mom asked.

Before I could answer, Nathan stepped into her line of sight and responded, "Those are from me, ma'am. I figured you and your daughter would love the beautiful addition to your beautiful home."

Now it was my mother's turn to become bashful. "Oh well thank you! I'm Mrs. Burke. And you are?"

"Nathan. It's my pleasure to meet you Mrs. Burke," he said as he reached his hand out to shake my mother's. "I live just on this street, about 8 houses down."

"Oh, are you Elena's son?"

Nathan responded, "Yes, that's me."

"That's great. It's nice to finally meet you. Well, I will leave you two be to get on with your plans. Have a nice night!" She disappeared to her bedroom.

"So are you ready to go?" asked Nathan, a seemingly smitten smile crossing his face. He was dressed in jeans and a t-shirt with a nice pair of pumas. His outfit put me at ease about mine, and I could feel the tension leave my shoulders.

"As ready as I'll ever be," I responded, smiling.

Since we lived close to a shopping center with a theater, we decided to walk and enjoy the nice weather. We talked about school and our families, and before we knew it, we were at the theater.

"So what would you like to see?" Nathan asked, subtly rubbing his palms on his jeans.

"I don't know," I responded. "I guess I didn't think that far ahead. I usually just come here by myself and randomly pick when I get here."

"Well how about something funny?" Nathan asked.

"Sure, why not. I'm up for anything."

He bought our tickets to some new comedy I had heard nothing about, and we headed in to find our seats. I followed him in and up towards the back where he chose two seats towards the middle, just the way I like it.

"Are these seats okay?" Nathan inquired.

"Yeah, they are actually perfect. This is about the same place I sit when I come," I replied.

We continued to talk until the previews started and then enjoyed the movie with quite a few laughs. At one point, his hand slid closer to mine, but he didn't make any moves beyond that.

The movie ended, and we proceeded back outside. I looked around at what was now darkness and shivered. I realized what I had forgotten thanks to my nerves: a jacket. I rolled my eyes at myself and turned to Nathan to see what he wanted to do.

"Are you up for grabbing a bite to eat?" Nathan asked. "I'm really in the mood for some steak and risotto if you're hungry."

"Actually, I am a little hungry now that I think about it. Do you have a place in mind?" I asked.

"I was thinking of this restaurant that's a little bit down the street. It's called 'The Butterfly Bistro.' It's incredibly charming and has a lot of options, so I thought it would be a good choice," he said as he made eye contact with me. I hoped he could see my excitement as I thought about the menu items at my favorite restaurant.

A shit-eating grin spread across my face as heat started to grow in my cheeks. "I would love that. I'll order their onion and mushroom tart. It's my favorite."

Nathan smiled, excited by my response. He grabbed my hand and led me back to the car, all but running as he did.

We arrived at the restaurant in under ten minutes and grabbed a table in the far corner, illuminated solely by twinkle lights and candles. It was romantic but comfortable, allowing us to talk without feeling too much of the romantic pressure.

"So, what are your plans for after high school?" I asked. I had come to find that most people my age hadn't figured out what they wanted for breakfast that morning, let alone what they wanted for their future.

"Well, I have a few colleges in mind, and I've already started prepping my early decision applications for my top colleges. What about you?" he responded.

I was pleasantly surprised and explained that I had already submitted most of my early admission applications. I anxiously fiddled with the napkin as I explained, unsure why I felt so nervous.

Nathan proceeded to ask me questions about my family life, my favorite things, and even what I wanted in the future out of a relationship. I explained to him that the loving relationship between my parents was always going to be my example and aspiration. My dad had always taught me that I deserve the most out of whomever I'm with and that I should never settle.

We were interrupted by the server who walked up with our entrées then sat in silence as we ate our delicious meals. While we were eating, I took the opportunity to look around the restaurant and people-watch.

I saw a couple that didn't look up from their phones, a group of friends laughing amongst themselves, and a woman with a glass of wine that looked like she had taken herself on a date and was thoroughly enjoying herself. I thought about the couple that wasn't even acknowledging one another and had to wonder if that was their regular routine. I couldn't imagine spending the money at a restaurant like this and not enjoying the ambiance.

I turned my attention back to Nathan, who quickly looked back down at his food.

"What?" I asked. I wondered if I had food in my teeth or had spilled on myself without realizing.

"Nothing," he said as he looked up blushing. "How is your food?"

"It's delicious as usual, you?" I asked.

"Same here. I love coming here, never disappoints," he said as he spooned another bite of risotto.

"I agree. I actually know the head chef." I replied, noting his expression light up at the knowledge. "Would you like to meet him? I can ask the server to see if he has some extra time?"

"Yes! I'd love to give him my compliments," he said excitedly.

Perfectly timed, the server came back over and I asked if he could see if Chef Monarch was available. Unfortunately he was elbow-deep in preparing some dishes, but Nathan was able to relay a message to him about the meal.

We finished our food and ate some macarons before Nathan paid for our meals and we left.

"Thank you for the movie and dinner. I had a really great time tonight," I said, under the assumption the date was over.

"Well I was actually really hoping to show you something before we went back home. But it's up to you of course," Nathan said shyly.

Now I was curious. Who was I to say no to the promise of mystery?

"Sure. Where is it?" I asked.

"It's on the way home. I won't keep you out too late," Nathan said as he wrapped his fleece-lined jacket around me.

"Oh I'm okay! You can keep your jacket!"

"No you're not. Don't act like I can't tell you're cold when you've been shivering and have goosebumps," he responded. "I have a long-sleeve anyway so I will be fine."

We walked to a park that was across the street from our neighborhood. As we walked along the grass, Nathan pulled out a flashlight from the jacket that I was wearing. He flashed the light in front of us as we walked.

As we approached the playground, he started to climb up the steps of the slide. Once he reached the top, he turned around and asked, "Are you coming?"

"Of course," I smirked as I quickly climbed to the top of the slide.

We went to the top of the playground and stood in silence for a few minutes, admiring the stars and moon. And, as cliché as it sounds, it really did feel like we were the only two people in the world. Nathan cleared his throat, which broke the silence.

"So what's going on? Why did you bring me here?" I asked, very curious about the intentions of this venture.

"Well, I wanted to show you this." He pointed the light towards a tree near the playground.

"I don't understand. I don't see anything."

"Look closely," he said.

I examined the tree he was shining the light at.

"I see the word 'no' —all caps—written on it?"

"Are you sure that's a 'no'?" he asked.

As I looked closer, I realized there was a plus sign between the two letters, like you see in the movies. Then it clicked, N+O meant Nathan plus Olivia. Not knowing what to think of this, I started to back away and asked, "Woah—what in the world? Why is this here?"

Nathan, looking frantic, responded, "Wait, please, just let me explain?"

I stopped in my tracks and gave him the chance to explain why our initials were sketched into a tree in our neighborhood park. I felt a sense of panic start to take over me, but I knew I needed to remain calm in case this was a worst-case scenario.

"I've had the biggest crush on you since the second grade, when I sat behind you in Mr. Theo's class. I was really nerdy, and because Greg Sullivan started a rumor that I had cooties, hardly anyone spoke to me. That totally flipped in high school. I grew out of my ugly duckling stage and started playing on varsity teams as a freshman." The color had drained from his face, and I could tell he was uncomfortable admitting all of these secrets.

His eyebrows furrowed as he paused, trying to read my expression. When he can't figure out what I'm thinking, he continues with his explanation.

"I went from one extreme of popularity to the other. And every time I see you in the hall or see you at one of my games, I want to talk to you. To let you know how I feel. And until a few days ago, I never thought that I would. If you hadn't fallen in front of me, I still don't think I would have. I probably would have gone forever not knowing what you might say back to me."

He stopped again and looked at me with a puppy-like gaze. I knew I had a confused look on my face as I found the resolve to confront what he told me. I was trying to think of a way to express myself without making him defensive, so I approached it in the best way I could.

"But why me? I'm nothing special. Why go through all of this trouble for me?" I asked.

"Are you kidding me? You don't realize just how much you have going for you, do you? You're one of the top students in our class. You've always been super funny and sweet, like the time during gym sophomore year where you were making jokes to put people at ease. And not to mention you're gorgeous. Anyone that doesn't see that is blind," he responded, and it was his turn to blush.

"But I still don't understand. Why have you never approached me up to now?"

"Because," he responded, "I was the one kid that everyone made fun of. Up to this point, I've never thought I had a chance with you. I know if I don't take this chance, I'll regret it for the rest of my life. I'm sorry if this is creepy. I understand if you just want to walk away right now."

The look in his eyes showed genuine care, and though normally a revelation of this kind should have frightened me, I didn't want to run away. Instead, I came up to him and put my head on his chest and my arms around his waist. Almost immediately, his arms closed gently, and I felt his warmth wrap around me.

After what seemed like hours in silence, Nathan grabbed my hand and led me back towards our houses. I thought he would have been happy that I had stayed, but his expression told me otherwise.

"What's wrong?" I asked, concerned.

"Why did you stay?" Nathan asked almost immediately. It was obvious this had been bothering him the last few minutes.

"Because you seem to be genuine, and not giving this a chance seems more risky than giving it one," I replied shakily. "I've always been terrified of the prospect of dating, and I think I also need to take this type of risk."

Nathan said nothing more and soon we were in front of my

house. I walked up the steps, half expecting him to follow me. He didn't. He stayed where he was, looking down at the ground, obviously still bothered by something.

"Are you sure there's nothing else you'd like to talk about?" I questioned.

"Yeah, I'm sure. Have a good night," he said as he abruptly turned away.

As I watched him walk down the path, I got the strange sense that he wasn't telling me the whole truth. But that wasn't something I could worry about at the moment. I opened my front door and stepped inside, finally escaping from the cold. As I was walking up to my room, I realized I was still wearing Nathan's sweater. I decided trying to track him down right now would not be productive and hung it up in my closet.

Once I got into the house, I grabbed my phone and called Emma to tell her about my date and how oddly it ended. She reassured me, saying I was likely just overthinking the situation, as I typically do. She helped me calm some of my anxiety through breathing exercises, and we went our separate ways for the night.

Getting ready for bed proved to be more difficult than usual. I couldn't focus on anything except for what was bothering Nathan. I hoped it was just his feelings about the fact that we were finally talking, and nothing that had to do with me.

Ch 3

The next two days were miserable. Despite Nathan giving me his jacket, I was now sporting a nasty cold. Luckily, I had my mom to take care of me. I've never done well when I get sick.

My mom came into my room with soup and extra blankets. "How are you feeling, honey?" she asked with noticeable concern.

"I still feel pretty crappy, but definitely better from when I woke up. Thank you for taking care of me," I responded.

My mother smiled. "Of course! What are mothers for?" she replied as she walked out of my room, closing the door behind her.

I was later awakened by the sound of knocking on my door. My mom peeped her head in to see if I was up and asked if I was up for a visitor.

Intrigued, I sat up and said sure, trying to think of who would come visit me.

A minute later, Nathan walked in with medicine and a baby giraffe stuffed animal, my favorite. I just looked at him, trying to drink in his black jeans and blue long-sleeved dress shirt that brought out the color in his eyes.

"What are you doing here?" I asked.

"Well I called your house phone since I hadn't heard from you in a couple of days, and I spoke with your mom. When she told me you were sick, I couldn't help but partially blame myself. So I figured I would bring a pick-me-up to try and cheer you up and hopefully make you feel better," he explained, blushing like he had a couple nights prior.

"Oh, well thank you. It definitely does help a lot. Your jacket is hanging up in my closet if you want to grab it?"

"I'll make sure to grab it before I leave," Nathan responded. "Is it okay if I sit on the end of your bed?"

I nodded, and he sat down at the end of my bed. We started talking, somewhat picking up from our conversation a couple nights before. First, we discussed our everyday lives, then we talked about our pasts. We learned that before moving to Oregon, we had lived in Washington, just north of Seattle in the nice town of Shoreline. We also had gone to the same school since kindergarten, but had not had a class together since second grade. It was crazy to think that we had never met previously, especially since our mothers had been friends for almost three years now.

"Isn't it crazy that we haven't really met until now?" I asked, curious as to why it took so long. "I just wonder why our moms never introduced us to each other."

"It's probably because I was never home, to be honest. I was always out for a club or for a sport. It's like I haven't been home for most of high school. And then during the summer, I go down to California to visit my family, and sometimes I go to sports camps. My crazy schedule was probably the problem," Nathan explained, shrugging.

"Eh, that's okay," I replied. "Better late than never, right?" I smiled, hoping to help ease the tension from the other night.

He smiled that gorgeous smile that seemed to dazzle me every time. I felt the heat rise as he responded, "Yes, that is very true. I'm very glad that it did happen."

The dizziness of my fever began to take over and I decided to lie down, still facing Nathan. He scooted himself up towards the top of the bed and started rubbing my back in circles. The sensation felt comforting as I allowed myself to loosen up the tension in my body.

We continued talking, not getting much deeper in our conversation. Though I felt I could trust Nathan, I was still scared to. I had so many secrets that I carried deep, deep within my heart, some that even my mother didn't even know. It seemed as if only an hour had passed, but it was getting late now, and I knew Nathan would have to leave soon. Still, I enjoyed the last few minutes of talking until he stood up and grabbed his jacket from my closet.

"I guess I have to get going," Nathan said, frowning.

"What's wrong?" I asked, knowing full well what his response was going to be.

"I'm just worried about you and don't want to leave you like this." His voice was shaking, like he was about to cry.

I stood up, walked to him, and put my arms around his waist. He immediately embraced me, kissing the top of my head. I didn't understand how I could feel so connected to someone I had just met, but it felt like nothing I had experienced before. It felt like the movies when they describe meeting your soulmate for the first time, though I didn't necessarily think it was the case here. We stood like this for a few minutes, and I let go, dreading his departure. My eyes started to well up with tears, and when he sensed something was wrong, he placed his fingers under my chin and lifted my eyes to his.

As if reading my mind, Nathan said, "I feel so connected to you. I know that this is quick, but I just feel like our connection is so strong. It almost feels unbelievable." He paused for a moment as he tried to read my face. "But I completely understand if you don't feel the same way."

I chose the words that followed carefully because while I felt connected with him, I was hesitant to be misleading in my feelings. We were so early on in whatever was developing that I didn't want to set any kind of expectations.

"I definitely feel a connection to you, and I'm definitely glad you are part of my life. I've needed the support," I said.

"I'll always be here for you, but only if it's what you want," Nathan said, tears glistening in his eyes.

I said nothing, unable to speak without bursting into tears. I let him out of my bedroom but couldn't walk any further because I was dizzy. I said good-bye and went to lie down in bed. Though I could feel the fatigue of my body setting in, my mind was wide-awake. Nathan's words kept going in circles through my mind. I couldn't help but wonder if he meant it, or if he was going to shatter me to pieces—like I had seen so many guys do to my friends. I had no more time to think about that as my mom entered my room with tea and more medicine.

"How are you feeling?" she asked, knowing she didn't just mean physically.

"I feel a little better. Having someone come visit definitely helped my mental state," I replied, anticipating the waves of questions that were bound to happen.

Instead, my mother just expressed her happiness that I was starting to feel better, set my tea and medicine down, and walked out of my room. I sat in shock as I took my medicine and drank the tea, wondering what had gotten into my mother. It was quite unlike her to not ask questions, especially about a boy. I didn't get to think about it long because I passed out from exhaustion within minutes.

Ch 4

By Monday, I was almost completely back to myself, with just a few sniffles left. I walked to my locker hoping to see Nathan before classes. I waited a few moments after the morning bell, and his absence from the hall felt like a kick in the gut.

I went through my whole day without seeing Nathan, and even on my walk home, he was nowhere to be found. While I had some frustration that he was not around, I couldn't ignore the pit that was forming in my gut. Had something happened to him? Or was he just blowing me off after all the things he had said to me?

When I got home, I climbed into bed, unable to stay awake, no thanks to my restless weekend. I passed out again, only waking to the sound of an emergency vehicle passing by the house.

I got out of bed, still groggy from my nap, and looked out my window to see what the commotion was about. I could see that flames had engulfed my neighborhood park, where not even a few days prior, Nathan had shared his feelings with me. I grabbed my sweater and ran downstairs to find my mother, but instead found an empty house. I went into the kitchen to grab water prior to heading outside. Before I could get to the refrigerator, there was a knock on the front door.

Looking through the peephole, I saw a police officer on the other side. My stomach dropped. Slowly, I opened the door for the officer, who was obviously distressed.

"Hello, Mrs. Burke?" he asked tentatively, knowing full well that I was not old enough to be Mrs. Burke.

"She's unavailable right now. May I ask what this is regarding?" I asked, my voice shaking.

"Who are you in relation to Mrs. Burke?" the officer asked.

"I'm her daughter. What's going on?" I was demanding now. I needed to know what had happened.

"I think we need to sit down to discuss this," the officer said, calmly.

I started to shake. Those are the words you dread when an officer is at your door. I could feel the tears welling up in my eyes as I walked the officer to the couch in the living room.

The officer told me there had been a fire in the neighborhood park. The very beginnings of the investigation suggested arson. He said my little brother was trapped on the playground and was unable to escape before the flames engulfed it.

"He's being rushed to Hillsboro Medical Center, but things aren't looking great right now," the officer continued, attempting to prepare me for the worst.

I was frozen from the inside, ice seeping into my veins with every additional word from his lips. I had nothing to say, nothing to feel. Emotions flew haphazardly from my body, silent as they dissipated. I thanked the officer and led him out of my house.

While I tried to let the news sink in, I walked back up to my room and sat on my bed. I stared at the wall watching the whites of my walls shift as they started to spin around me. I took a moment, put on my shoes, then grabbed my phone and headphones and ran downstairs and out of the house.

I sprinted down the street with my headphones in, waiting for the tears to come down. But they didn't. I had felt my consciousness leave my body with the arrival of the officer. An hour later, I realized I was still running and stopped, breathless.

I didn't recognize where I was, but I knew I wasn't in my neighborhood anymore. Goosebumps went down my spine as I shivered. I checked the GPS on my phone. I was almost 6 miles away from my house. Oddly, I had not heard anything from anyone in that time, which made me that much more concerned.

I started the jog back home. As my feet gained traction, I could feel eyes on me. Something was wrong. I glanced backwards and saw nothing. I jogged for about half a mile more before I turned around and saw someone duck behind a corner.

Just as I was grabbing my pepper spray from my waistband, I bumped into someone, nearly scaring myself to death. I looked up to see whom I had bumped into and apologized, coming face to face with Nathan.

"Are you okay?" he asked.

Without responding, I turned around to find my "stalker," but they had long disappeared. I turned back to look at Nathan, who was staring in the direction I had turned.

"What was that about?"

"Nothing," I responded. "What are you doing out here?"

"Your mom told me that you weren't home, and no one could get a hold of you, so I came to look for you. I know what happened to your brother. Are you doing okay?"

I looked at him, his blue eyes looking into mine, and wondered where he had been the last few days. "Where have you been? You completely disappeared off the map, and now you come out of nowhere to be the hero? That's not how this works."

"What do you mean?" Nathan asked, genuine concern crossing his face

"I mean that I looked forward to seeing you today, and even after you promised you'd be there for me, you weren't. Why, what happened?" The tears were streaming down my face as I choked the words out. I couldn't take it anymore. My baby brother was in the hospital, and I wasn't even there for him. Yet, here I was, irrationally worried about the fact that Nathan hadn't been at school.

"I'm sorry, Olivia. I dropped the ball today. I took a personal day. I'm so sorry I wasn't there for you when you needed it most. I know you probably don't believe me, but I was about to call you to see if I could help at all." This time the tears fell from his eyes down his face as he reached out to put his arms around me and pull me in.

I stood there for a minute bawling into his arms as I thought about what I needed to do. I backed out of Nathan's grip and looked up at him. Without saying anything, I put my headphones on and sprinted away towards my house. I needed to go to the hospital to see my little brother. I needed to make sure he was okay.

As I got back to the house, another cop was pulling up. I stopped in my tracks and turned toward the cop that was slowly climbing out of his cruiser.

"Olivia Burke?" The cop questioned.

"Yes?" I responded, dread sticking to me like wet newspaper.

"I was given orders to escort you to the hospital."

"May I drive in my car and just follow your cruiser?" I asked, not wanting to be stranded at the hospital.

"Of course, I'd be happy to lead you to the hospital."

I quickly ran into the house, changed my shirt and grabbed a jacket and my car keys. I ran back down the stairs and out the door to the driveway.

As I turned on my car, I could see Nathan quickly approaching the house from down the street. I backed out and turned down the street just in time to have him approach my window. I rolled it down and asked him what he wanted.

"Please let me come with you so I can make today up to you," he said, face full of desperation

"No."

And with that, I drove away to see my little brother.

The officer was definitely not going the speed limit most of the way, for which I was very thankful. As we pulled into the hospital, I could see my mom's car front and center of the valet. I pulled up, leaving my keys in the ignition as I got out.

"Could I please have a ticket so I can go into the hospital?" I asked, trying to steady my voice.

"Yes ma'am. Here is your ticket. Please be sure to keep that so that we know which car is yours."

"Thank you, I will." Taking the ticket from his hand, I ran through the front doors of the hospital.

Thankfully the front desk was 20 feet from the entrance, and my run turned into a brisk walk as I approached the women at the front desk.

"How may we help you," one of the women asked.

"I'm looking for my little brother, William Burke."

"It looks like he's in the pediatric wing of the ICU. Room 209A. Do you know how to get over there?"

"I think so. Thank you." I continued with my frenzied walk to find my brother.

I reached the second floor of the building, and I felt my heart drop as I passed the children's cancer center. I already had a hatred for hospitals, and seeing the cancer center caused me to relive a part of my past that I would have preferred to forget.

I followed the signs to room 209A. I took a deep breath. As I took a step into the room, I felt a hand on my shoulder. I turned, half expecting to see Nathan. Instead, it was my mother, face swollen, tear stains visible on her cheeks. All I could do was embrace her as tightly as I could. I whispered to her that it would be okay, even though I didn't believe the words myself. Her body started to shake as I held her close to me, so I walked her into the room to let her slump into the chair. She curled up, her body contorting to fit the chair, and fell fast asleep within minutes.

I turned to look at my brother. He was covered in gauze and bandages, and there wasn't much of him I could see. He was intubated, and I could see the machines working hard to keep him alive.

I sat in my brother's room for a bit to keep watch over my mom. After about an hour, I got up to seek out a doctor on my brother's case. I went to the nurses' station and asked for an available physician, and she said she would be sure to page them over as soon as they were available.

Instead of walking back to the room, I decided to let my mother sleep and walked around the hospital instead. As I looked around the pediatric wing, I found it to be inspiring, despite all of the sick and injured children. There were paintings and drawings that the children had made, saying what they would be when they grew up. Though for some of them, it wouldn't be possible, it gave them hope that anything could happen. It gave them hope to fight the battle rather than giving up. And that's exactly what they needed, which I had learned first-hand.

After about 30 minutes of wandering about the hospital, I headed back to the room, where I found my mother still sound asleep, clearly needing the rest.

I sat down in a chair and turned on some Grey's Anatomy, feeling it suited the situation well. Within minutes of turning the show on, I had fallen asleep. But this was not a restful sleep. It was quite the opposite, in fact. I had a nightmare about the fire, large flames blazing all around the playground, seeing a silhouette of a man that looked familiar. When I awoke, I couldn't quite pinpoint who the person was, but it left me uneasy.

I quickly stood up, causing myself a head rush. I paused, allowing my head to catch up to the rest of my body, and walked back towards the nurses' station. As I approached, I realized there was no one at the desk. I stood and waited for a few minutes, but no one came around, so I went back to the room. I watched some more Grey's Anatomy, desperately trying to stay awake so I could speak with the doctor when he came in.

As I felt myself dozing off again, I heard a man's voice say, "Mrs. Burke?"

I stood up and reached my hand out and said, "No sir, Ms. Burke. Are you the doctor taking care of my brother, Will?"

The doctor's hand met mine as he introduced himself. "Yes I

am. My name is Dr. Fergusson. Would you like to step outside so as to not wake your mother?" he asked, clearly hiding his concern.

"That would be great," I responded, forcing a smile.

We walked outside of the room, and the doctor stopped and turned towards me. "What do you know of your brother's condition?"

"I don't know much except that he was an alleged victim of arson and that things weren't looking good when they were bringing him to the hospital."

Something was clearly wrong. The look in the doctor's eyes was not that of confidence. Dr. Fergusson hesitated as he drew a deep breath in to tell me the news. "Your brother suffered severe smoke inhalation. But unfortunately, that's not the only thing we found. He is severely burned on 70 percent of his body. He also had an aneurysm deeply rooted in his brain stem that must have ruptured during the frenzy of trying to get him to the hospital. The prognosis is not looking good." He looked up from his clipboard trying to read my face.

Instead, I looked him dead in the eye and responded, "So what does this mean?"

"He's in a medically induced coma right now. We are trying to get the bleeding to stop. But, unfortunately, there is no sign of stoppage just yet."

I thought I was fine, but the darkness overtook me as I must have come crashing to the ground.

I woke up, dazed and confused about where I was. I could see the hospital walls as I opened my eyes and shot up in bed. I looked at my right arm and, sure enough, there was an IV sticking out of it in all its glory. I couldn't understand why I was in a hospital bed when I was there for my brother.

I turned towards the door just in time to see a nurse passing by, but even with my calling for her, she didn't seem to hear me. I looked around my bed to find the nurse call button hanging from the same side as my IV. I grabbed the chord and pressed the button, expecting to wait a few minutes before I would see any personnel. But within seconds, in came the nurse that had just passed by my room not seconds before.

"What do you need?" She asked rudely.

"I'm just trying to figure out what happened to me. I don't know why I'm in this hospital bed."

"Well, you passed out and hit your head. Clearly you're concussed," she continued with her bitchy attitude.

"I'm sorry, but did I do something to you to deserve this rude treatment from you? Because as far as I know, I haven't even talked to you," I responded, done with beating around the bush.

The nurse, shocked, looked at me with a seemingly newfound respect. "I apologize for coming off rudely. It's just been an insane night in the emergency room. We just had a kid, looks to be in middle school, who came in severely injured from a fire on a playground near the school."

Not realizing that this kid was my brother, she looked up and saw the devastation that became evident on my face. "Oh no, what did I say?" She asked, the look of concern growing rapidly.

"I, just, is he going to be okay?" Tears were welling in my eyes as I choked the words out.

Before she answered me, she looked over at the whiteboard hanging in my hospital room. Her face went white as she turned to face me. "That's your brother, isn't it?"

I lost it. I completely lost it. The tears were pouring down my face as I stared blankly at the windows in front of me. I couldn't breathe, and I heard the nurse's voice drift away as the darkness overtook me again.

Ch 6

The next few days were a blur. While my brother fought for his life, doctors were trying to figure out why I kept passing out and why my bloodwork was off. I hadn't heard from Nathan, and I wasn't sure if it is because he didn't want to be with me in the hospital or if he was giving me space. Either way, I had bigger things to worry about.

Emma had called me to check in. I tried not to fall apart at the seams while I told her of the devastation that surrounded me. While I appeared outwardly successful, my insides felt like they were crumbling. I had dealt with so much in such little time without truly getting to process it the way I needed to. I hated pretending I was "fine" to my best friend, but I knew in this moment it was for the best.

I finally had a chance to get out of my hospital bed, and the first place I went was my brother's room. There he was, intubated with so many tubes and wires and such protruding from him. I bent by his bedside and wept. My little brother, who I had grown so close to, who I had spent time playing sports with, teaching math to, and doing everything I could to make sure he was protected, was lying there, appearing lifeless.

I wasn't religious, but in that moment, I prayed and hoped that my baby brother would make it through this. There was nothing else I could do. I cried some more and grabbed his hand, helplessly hoping

I would feel movement.

I walked out of the room to continue my journey of looking around the hospital. I walked past the baby and infant NICU and watched as parents were losing their dear children before even getting the chance to watch them grow up.

I started questioning things. Would that be better or worse than losing your child when they are older? Is it easier to bury a baby or your teenager or adult? As someone who had to watch their father be buried just years before, I started to doubt the faith I had in the world that something better was out there.

Back to the room I went, still questioning things. I turned the corner to my room to find my mother standing there, staring into space.

"Mom? Are you okay?" I asked, knowing full well how stupid that question was.

But she made it seem like she was just fine, acting as if nothing was going on. "I'm good honey, how are you feeling? The doctors said you seemed to be making progress with your appetite and walking around."

I had been on appetite stimulants and pain medication for having hurt my head and arms on the way down each time I passed out, so my improvements were more medical than they were mentally. But I wasn't going to let my mom know that with everything she was going through.

"Have you heard anything about my results yet? Or anything

new about Will and his progress?" I asked these questions, hoping for the best but expecting the worst.

"Nothing yet honey, but I will be sure that you are updated as soon as I find out anything. I'm going to go back to Will's room, do you need anything before I do?"

I looked at those eyes of the beautiful woman standing in front of me, seeing nothing but pain and the desire to hide it, so I told her that I didn't need anything and would let the nursing staff know if I did. I hugged her, told her how much I loved her, and reciprocated my desire to help her in any way she needed. She meandered back towards the ICU as I turned to go into my room.

I sat down in my hospital bed, desperate for relief for my family. Why couldn't it be me? My mom had already gone through so much. Why our family? These thoughts enveloped my mind as I passed back out, likely from the amount of narcotics and sleeping aids running through my system.

I awoke what felt like hours later to a havocked code blue. My nurse was in my room, and I asked where that code blue was happening. She looked at me, sure to hide any clues to what was going on and said, "I believe it is in the children's section, but I am not 100% certain."

She left, and I was alone in my thoughts again. I got up, grabbed my IV stand and walked toward my brother's room. A mass of people were frantically swarming at the end of the hallway. I grabbed my stand and lifted my gown so I could get some speed. Once

I got closer, I realized it wasn't my brother's room, but rather the child next door. While I felt the relief, I also felt the grief for the family inside of that room, praying that their little girl would make it. I raised my hand to my face and closed my eyes. When I opened them, I was in my hospital bed again.

"Oh sweetie, you had an anxiety attack and then you collapsed into a seizure right outside of your brother's room. The doctor's think your body is just exhausted from all of the things you have been going through, so it's needed recovery for these last few weeks." This nurse was so kind and genuine, so I reached out to give her a hug, which she gladly gave back.

Weeks?.

"I've been here for a few weeks? How many days exactly?" I was trying to figure out how long I had been there as I had only felt like I had been there a few days, not weeks.

"I'd have to check your chart to be certain, but I want to say this is the start of week six?" she said, seemingly unaware that I had no idea what had transpired over that time.

I could not even begin to believe that I had been there for so long.

"Have I had any visitors other than my mom?"

"No honey, just some cards and flowers from some classmates and teachers. Were you expecting anyone? We can try to get a hold of them?" she asked, so sweetly. But I denied her request. If Nathan didn't want to come see me on his own, I didn't want to see him.

43

"How did my tests come out??" I had been wondering about them since I had woken up earlier, but hadn't thought to ask about them once the emergency happened in pediatrics.

"Well, we have discovered you have some anemia and hypoglycemia. Other than that, all of your results from bloodwork and imaging looked normal." the nurse said, seeming to hope to relieve some of my stress.

The sound of my mom's concerned voice wafted through the door. I mustered the strength and got up to see what was going on.

As soon as I stepped outside of the door to my room, they both fell silent, turning to where I was standing. I knew better than to ask what was going on with those cues, so I just asked for some apple juice and went to lay back down.

Ch 7

Heavy breathing. Sweat pouring. The inability to move. This was sleep paralysis. I hadn't had it in years, not since the time surrounding my father's death. Why was this happening?

I knew I was in my hospital bed, and that I was not alone. Darkness radiated from the corners of the room. I shifted my eyes to see a dark figure emerge opposite the door. My chest started expanding rapidly and relentlessly. Fighting sleep paralysis is pointless, so I prayed for my consciousness to fully awaken. I was trying to take deep breaths with my eyes closed to calm myself but was overwhelmed with the smell of smoke and the sting of heat on my skin. Flames surrounded the figure's feet, but they didn't burn.

Suddenly, I realized that the figure had been standing with its arms behind its back as it started moving one arm in front of itself. I looked towards its hand, and there was a match in it. It was unlit, but larger than a usual match, causing more uneasiness. The figure slowly lifted its hand to its face, and just as it had reached eye level, it caught fire, illuminating a pair of soulless eyes.

"No!" I screamed to the dark figure in the corner. I had a suspicion that it was my brother's alleged assailant.

I regained motor control, overwhelmed by palpitations and a drenched hospital bed. The figure vanished, and I was left to be alone with my thoughts. But not for long because I had apparently choked out my scream, as there was a nurse and doctor at the foot of my bed within an instant of me waking up.

"Are you okay honey?" asked the nurse, with genuine concern for my well-being.

I explained that I was fine and had just woken up from a nightmare. But in reality, I was wondering what I had just witnessed. Had I just had a vision of the person that put my brother in a coma? My childhood had been filled with these types of foretelling visions. I hadn't experienced them in a long time and figured they had been left behind with my adolescence. I didn't have enough time to make sense of it because my mom came running in.

"Olivia! What happened? Are you okay?"

She was scrambling and panicked. She looked like she had just seen a ghost.

"I'm fine mom, I just woke up from a nightmare. Are you okay?" I asked, noticing how sickly she looked after the last few weeks she had endured. She brushed me off, saying she was fine, but I still didn't believe her. Her plate was already overflowing, so I didn't push my concern .

We spent the next few hours talking about random things and watching Grey's Anatomy. It was nice to spend some time with my mom and forget about recent events, even if it was short-lived.

"Mom, can we go see Will? I think I may need your help so I don't fall or pass out again, but I'd really like to go see him."

"Of course, honey. I'm happy to get you over there. Let's just use the wheelchair."

I was happy to oblige even though I hated being in the wheelchair. It made me feel like I was not able to manage even the simplest of tasks. But since it made my mom feel better, I happily obliged.

I grabbed my fluids, hung them on the pole of the wheelchair, and sat down with my feet propped on the rests. My mom proceeded to push me through the hospital, and as we were passing by the elevators, I asked her to take me down to the gift shop. I felt guilty, like I had betrayed Will by being unconscious for so long. I wanted to give him something to remind him that his big sister was always by his side. A little stuffed elephant stared at me from behind the shop window. Not only was it his favorite animal, but it represented strength, which is something we all needed.

We got back on the elevator and headed over to Will's room. My mom pushed me up right next to his bed so that I could be within reach of him. We talked to Will, reassuring him that we would be by his side. It seemed to also reassure us in the moment.

I looked up at my mom, and she looked disheveled, frustrated, and like she hadn't gotten a good night's rest in months. My chest collapsed knowing the exacerbated pain my mom was feeling after everything we'd been through over the last few years, but I needed to be strong for her.

"Mom, why don't you head home and get a good shower,

some food, and a nice night in your own bed? I know you need it, so please don't argue with me on it."

She looked up at me with bloodshot eyes as she sat silent for a moment. "You know what honey? That actually sounds like a really great idea. There's not much more I can do here, and you will be here if anything changes with Will. I do want to ask, though, how would you feel about me going back to work? I am nearing the end of my FMLA, and while my company has been great and understanding, I don't want to risk losing our insurance and income. Do you think you could handle that? I'm hoping you will be out of here soon, too, so you can at least get back to school and finish out the year."

"Of course, mom," I responded. "I would be happy to take over as much of the responsibility as I can. I know this can't be easy for you, especially after dad. So whatever I can do to help, just let me know."

She swiped away the wetness in her eyes. After gathering her things and giving me a hug, she reached over to Will. Whispering something I couldn't hear, she kissed his barely exposed forehead and left.

I looked back at my brother, taking in all of the devices that were keeping his poor little body alive. He was covered in fresh bandages from his most recent skin graft. The parts of him I could see were raw and an angry red color. He looked nothing like the gentle boy who was my brother.

"I'm so sorry," I choked out before starting to bawl. "I'm so sorry I let this happen to you and didn't protect you. I wish I could take it all back, I wish I could have been there. I wish you could have been home," I said as I laid my head on his hospital bed and cried into the elephant.

Ch 8

Some time later, I felt movement. I lifted my head to hold his hand. "Will, can you hear me?" His hand moved again, and I shrieked with excitement as I realized that my brother was squeezing his hand around mine.

The doctor and nurse ran in asking what had happened.

"He squeezed my hand! I asked if he could hear me, and I felt it tighten!!"

They asked me to move so they could do some testing on his eye reactivity and tried to duplicate his hand movement, but to no avail. His pupils were still nonreactive, and they weren't able to get a response from his hand. I tried again, pleading with Will to show us some sign of life, but I was unable to get anything beyond a natural body twitch.

"Olivia, we need to discuss some things with you and your mother. Is she available?" the doctor asked. I knew something was terribly wrong. This wasn't a good sign, and his subtle demeanor told me that I should prepare for bad news.

"Let me call her and see what her schedule looks like."

I took a minute to compose myself as I didn't need my mom to know something was wrong until she came in so she could focus on the rest of her day and safely getting to the hospital.

The phone rang and rang until I finally reached her voicemail. The familiar, robotic *Thank you for calling, please leave a message after the tone and we will get back to you shortly* rang through my ears so loudly that I almost didn't hear the tone and hesitated as I left a message for my mother.

"Hey mom, the doctor's have some things to discuss with you, and I just wanted to, uhm, know what your schedule looked like for you to come in. Just call or text and let me know so that I can give them a good idea of when you're going to be here."

Just as I hung up the phone, in walked my mom, seemingly in a chipper mood, which made my heart drop that much harder. She walked into my brother's room full of hope that was about to be ripped from her grasp.

"Hi honey! How are you feeling? I know I was here just this morning but I wanted to check up during my lunch break. After six weeks here with you, I just can't seem to keep myself away" she said with a soft smile.

I opened my mouth as Dr. Ferguson walked into Will's room with an outstretched hand, "Mrs. Burke, how are you doing today?" He covered her hand with his other hand, gripping tightly as to be reassuring. But I knew that her world was about to come crashing down. I wasn't sure what the news was going to be exactly, but I knew it couldn't be good based on the demeanors that I had been surrounded by that afternoon.

"We need to discuss some things with you about Will's case,

do you mind coming with us down the hall?"

"Of course, can my daughter come with us?" Her arm wrapped around my shoulders

"I think it would be best if we just discuss things first, if that's okay? We have some very important decisions to make, and it usually is easier with just one family member at a time."

She agreed, rather tentatively, but knew that was the best decision at that moment. I watched as the doctors took my mother away to discuss what was almost guaranteed to be bad news about my brother's progression, or lack thereof.

A nurse walked in as I turned back to Will, and all I wanted to do was ask what was wrong with my brother. What decision was so important that it couldn't be discussed in front of me? What could they possibly be hiding? I was already in poor condition — it wasn't as if any bad news would be a surprise at this point.

I turned the TV on to watch reruns of the first season of Will's favorite show, 13 Reasons Why. I had read that book long ago, and was elated when they had made it a show. It showed the troubles of mental health and its causes, as well as gave me and Will even more to bond around.

Both Will and I had our mental health demons, myself more so due to my age at my father's death. We appreciated the light it brought to the subject and for the opportunity to see relatable characters on-screen. While there continues to be a lot of controversy around the show, we appreciated it for what it was worth. Inspired by the plights of the characters, we were able to have a very serious conversation with our mom. While it broke her heart a little, she was happy that we wanted to have that conversation with her rather than handle our pain on our own. We watched the show over again with our mom and just sat in a heap on the couch, crying, letting out all of the emotions we had all pent up since my father's death.

I must have drifted off because I woke up to the doctor and my mom walking back into Will's room. Dazed, I asked for an update, thinking my mom would want to let me know what was going on. But, instead, she had the nurse take me back to my room. I was stunned, not because she sent me back to my room, but because she didn't want to trust in me to help her. I didn't understand. Had I done something wrong? I started questioning myself, wondering why my own mom didn't want to let me know what was happening with my baby brother. As the nurse pushed me in my wheelchair, I felt pressure behind my eyes and my face start to heat.

We got back to my room where the nurse helped me back into my bed. She asked if I wanted the TV on, which I declined. I just wanted to continue to sleep this nightmare away. So I closed my eyes, and drifted off in hopes of doing so.

"Who are you?" I asked the dark figure standing in front of me. I got no response, but I turned to feel the flames from the park. "What happened here?" I asked, more to myself, but this time, I got an answer.

"Someone set this place aflame, you didn't see it happen?" the figure asked. I didn't know what to say. A simple no wouldn't suffice, but neither would an explanation I didn't have.

"I didn't, did you?" I turned to see the figure gone from sight. I turned towards the head and inhaled thick, black smoke. It billowed all around me, and then, a scream.

Will? Was that you? I couldn't see anything as I drowned on the thick, black smoke that filled my lungs.

I woke to chaos and noise all around me. I could hear heavy running down the hall, and panic in the nurse and doctors' voices as they placed paddles on my chest. I called out to tell them it wasn't necessary, and that I was awake. Why couldn't I move? What was happening? Then, suddenly, I could feel my body start to compulse and my eyes roll back as I fell to the darkness again.

I awoke, able to feel the tubes in my throat and wires connected all over my body to keep me alive. I imagined what I would look like to my mom, and shuddered in horror. I tried to open my eyes and move my hands, then started to panic.. It was as if I was seeing myself from someone else's perspective.

"What's wrong with her?" A voice all too familiar distracted me from my panic, as I wondered the same.

"Honestly Mrs. Burke, we don't know. All of her scans have been clear for her brain, and we've run just about every blood test that is covered by insurance."

"Then run the ones that aren't covered. I cannot lose my husband and then both of my kids a few years later. You have to do something!" she was screaming in agony at this point, and all I wanted to do was hug and comfort her. I focused on my hands to try summoning all of my energy to reach out to her. I drifted back off, with dread slowly enveloping me.

I hear crying. Am I dreaming again? I can't tell. But I do recognize the voice talking to me, even if I can't pinpoint it.

"It's nice here, isn't it honey?"

Honey? Who, even in my dreams, was calling me honey? Was it the nurse? The only people that had ever called me that were my parents, but my mom had stopped calling that after my dad died. Could it be? I opened my eyes to see familiar deep blue-green eyes looking at me, his beautiful brunette locks wondrously wisping around them. We embrace, my immobility forgotten in an ethereal body. My face contorts with the force of my smile.

"Daddy!" I screamed as I held him tighter. The cologne I had smelled for years when he was alive wafted into my nostrils, and I felt the flannel between my fingers as I squeezed him tighter in response. I didn't want this moment to end, but then I realized, I was seeing my father, five years after his death. "Where are we?" My sheer panic was evident, but my dad just embraced me tighter.

"You're safe now, baby. You're safe."

He used a soothing voice, but the question of my mortality remained in the air. I missed him terribly, but I wasn't ready to be dead. I had Will and mom waiting for me. I pulled away to take in our surroundings. There was an angelic, bright, and colorful presence permeating the air. And there were no solid shapes or distinguishable forms, other than my dad. "Dad, I'm so sorry, but I'm not ready to be here yet. Mom needs me. She's been a mess since you've been gone."

"Oh honey, I wish I could change things. I've missed you and Will and your mom dearly. I truly hope you know that."

He brought his forehead to mine. Tears started falling down both of our faces as we came to the realization that neither of us were ready to lose the other, and it was about to happen again. I'm a fighter, and his tears told me he knew that. But that wouldn't stop us from taking what little time we had together.

"How about Will, honey? How has he been doing? I know he was struggling in school before I left. Has he gotten the hang of it?."

Fresh tears emerged at the same time he reached to wipe them away. I didn't know what to say. How do I tell my father, who has been dead for five years, that my family has done nothing but struggle since his passing, with me holding it together at the seams?

"Oh dad, so much has happened these last few years. Where do I start??"

"The beginning. Don't skip anything.."

I started from day one after he left us. That was the only way I could keep timelines straight and be able to tell him everything. I told him about mom's struggle to keep weight on her body due to her depression, her anxiety medication creating more issues with that, and how she just couldn't keep her head up. I told him how she lost her job and went on unemployment for two years and lived off the money from his life insurance.

"You know one thing she never failed to do though? Even on her worst days? She was always there for us, no matter what. It's like she mustered your strength to make sure that we were okay, even though she wasn't. But exactly two and a half years after you died, she snapped out of it. She got her dream job, and now she is the happiest I have seen her in a long time. I know she still struggles with you gone, but I think Will being your spitting image helps her get through the dark times."

His eyes welled, and I could tell that he felt guilty, but also comforted, by the turn in my mother. And now I was about to break his heart.

"Daddy, I miss you so much." My face was dry. I was angry now. I was angry that he was taken away from me so early in life. But I was even angrier that Will didn't get to know the wonderful man in front of me the way I did. I cherished the days I had with him because I was old enough to feel his love and guidance. I don't know if Will was too young to understand the slow deterioration of his father, or if his childhood innocence was working overtime to protect him, but he didn't seem to understand the severity of the situation until he realized our dad was no longer there. Now, I was either going to lose him again, or Will was going to lose me. But I couldn't let the latter happen because I knew I was better equipped to lose my dad again than Will was to lose me.

I turned to my dad, ready to tell him about Will.

"What about you, Olivia? Tell me about you. Are you still getting out on the green?"

I hesitated, then told him about taking care of mom and keeping my grades up. "I had a tutor for about a year and a half. But they were there more to help me focus than they were there to teach me anything. I also joined the soccer team, and the golf team has definitely kept me out on the green. I am thankful for the much needed distractions."

A shadow flashed through his eyes as he tried to process why I needed a distraction. "Oh honey, that's great! Is it still winter season for soccer and spring for golf? I miss playing golf with you and our competitions we used to have. I think about those often."

Ignoring his sentiments, I changed the subject. "So, are you pretty conscious of your life on Earth from here? You talk about things like you remember everything pretty vividly." I was curious about the extent of his memories, but I was also curious if he was able to know things beyond his memory. Was he able to know what was going on with our family now that he was gone?

"I remember most things pretty well. The only gap I have is the 3 months before I died. I don't remember much about those days. I try to, but I usually just end up frustrated and focus on what I do remember." He went on to tell me about how he spent the first bit of time after his death wondering what was happening and why he couldn't see us. After his memories started to return, he realized he'd never be coming home.

I listened intently with wide eyes. He had been through so much, just like us. "Are you able to see anything at all with what has happened beyond your death? Or is that not allowed or whatever?"

59

"Unfortunately not," he answered. I could see him switch gears to think about that, but I had to interrupt him as I didn't know how much time I had left with him. He had to know about Will before we were separated.

"Dad, there's something you need to know. It's about Will."

Concern washed across his face as he realized that something was wrong. "What is it, honey? What's happened?"

I had no clue how to tell him his son was in the hospital on his deathbed, as he stood before his daughter who was clearly sharing the same fate. I opened my mouth as his figure began to fade.

"Dad!" I called out. His eyes reached mine as his form vanished.

Ch 10

I was awake now. Actually awake. Eyes open, I witnessed my mom cry out in relief that I was out of my coma.

I tried to speak, but immediately started choking on the tubes coming out of my mouth. The nurse came running in after hearing my mom scream for help. As delicately as she could, she pulled the tube from deep within my esophagus. It was incredibly painful, and I coughed up a little blood as a result.

"Wha-what happened?" I stuttered. "Why was I in a coma?"

"Oh honey, you had a few seizures so they put you into a coma again to let your body rest. Unfortunately, it seems your body didn't catch back up the first time during three of those weeks. The seizures were caused by a clotting disorder that they discovered. We should be able to put you on some medication for it and hopefully control it from happening again. It will take some trial and error, but we will figure it out together," she said while cracking a smile. She reached out and put her hand on mine. "I'm so sorry all of my focus has been on Will. I didn't realize just how sick you were until they had to put you into the coma. Can you forgive me?"

Tears were welling up in her eyes again. I thought of Dad, and I couldn't help but cry with her. "Yes, of course mom. Things have been moving so fast, and you've done your best. No one can fault you for that. Speaking of which, how is Will doing?"

A wail emerged from her lips at his name. She was crying so hard and so loudly that an unfamiliar nurse hastily pulled her away to have a breather. The nurse returned and came right up to my bedside. "Your brother is dying, Olivia. Your mother has made the decision to pull him from his vents and let him go so his organs can be donated. Sorry to be the one to tell you."

She was blunt and to the point, but she was not sorry. She reveled in being the one to tell me. She showed no sympathy or empathy for me or my mother, and it was evident from the moment she grabbed my mother by the arm to take her from the room. She wasn't there to comfort either of us. She wanted to give me that news, she wanted to see the pain in my eyes as I found out my brother was going to be taken away from me.

The unprofessionalism was astonishing, and I couldn't believe what I was hearing, not only in her verbiage, but in her tone.

"Get the fuck out!" I screamed. I was furious. I wasn't going to accept her treatment, and now she knew it. She didn't move so I screamed at her again, asking for the head nurse. She scoffed as she smirked and left my room.

An hour had gone by, and the head nurse still hadn't come in, so I pressed the nurse's button on my remote. Within moments, my favorite nurse—the one with true empathy—entered the room. She started to ask if I was alright and then saw the gaunt terror that had remained on my face. She rushed to my bed and held me in comforting arms while cooing soothing words in my ear. Her motherly embrace gave a moment's comfort before she pulled away.

I explained what had happened with the previous nurse, and I asked if she could help me file a complaint. She readily agreed and said she would write a report while I got some rest.

"Thank you," I whispered as I closed my eyes. I just wanted everything to go away. And so it did when I drifted off as the nurse put my anxiety and pain medication into the IV.

Ch 11

The park is on fire. The heat cracks at my exposed skin as I move closer. What were my dreams trying to tell me? What could I learn here, if I wasn't there at the time of the attack? Because if I had been, Will's organs wouldn't be getting divied up right now.

I started kneeling by the edge of the playground area as I saw the tarp on top of the set aflame. I look down at my hands as I set them on the ground, but they aren't my own. They are someone else's. And based on the size and hair, I would guess a man's hands. But I couldn't be sure as the air had grown dark and thick .

Was I being sent a message? Was I slowly discovering who had committed such a heinous crime against my neighborhood and brother, piece by piece? I heard footsteps nearby, but then I shifted into a different scene. It's mine and Nathan's first date where he showed me the tree with our initials. A spark cracked within the trunk, illuminating them. I could feel my body start to float as the memories of Nathan started to flow back to me. I missed him, I missed his smell, I missed his lips on mine, but only the wistful imagined phantom of what they may feel like. But what I missed most was his presence in my life, the comfort he provided.

I awoke to uncontrollable shaking as I realized that I hadn't acknowledged my feelings towards Nathan going MIA for the last couple of months. I was angry. I threw one of my pillows to the ground, nearly ripping out my IV as I screamed into the other one.

Why had he abandoned me? Why hadn't he at least called or texted to see how I was doing? Did he even know that I had ended up in the hospital too? The relentless thoughts halted when my mom walked into the room.

She picked up my pillow, and placed it on the end of my bed, no questions asked. If she knew I was upset, she didn't show it.

"Olivia, I have some news to share with you," she choked out as she grabbed my hand. "I will be taking William off of his life support in two days, once we find the final recipients of his organs." My diaphragm seized as the words left her mouth, hearing this news for the second time. I couldn't believe this was an option for her, and so quickly, too, especially after everything we had been through with my father. She had fought tooth and nail to keep him alive, why wouldn't she do the same for Will?

"Mom, have you gotten second opinions? You're really just going to let him go after he squeezed my hand?"

"Honey, I don't want to arg- wait. What did you just say?" she asked, her face losing color.

"I asked why you would just let him go after he squeezed my hand the other day in response to me talking to him. I just don't understand how you could give up on him so quickly."

Her look of concern and sadness quickly changed into one of anger. Without a word, she marched out of my room and down the hall. Alerting the whole hospital with her high voice, she called for

Will's doctor. The poor, unsuspecting man attempted to reason with her, but my mother's rise in pitch took no prisoners. She vehemently demanded to know why she wasn't told about Will's movement. I could tell by his tone that he was just as in the dark as she was. He walked into my room, and as I saw him, I realized it wasn't the same doctor that was on the hospital floor the day Will had squeezed my hand.

"Olivia, when did Will squeeze your hand? Are you sure it wasn't just an involuntary twitch?"

"It was a few days ago, didn't the doctor or nurse tell you? Or at least put it in his chart?" I asked, very concerned at what else they could have missed regarding my brother's health.

"I'm going to go back and reread, but I truly, honestly don't remember any notations of it," he explained as he walked out of my room, replaced by my mother walking into it.

She looked at me, clearly abashed. "That was not a proud moment for me. I'll be sure to apologize to him."

"It's okay, mom. I'm sure he knows you are under a lot of stress with everything going on right now." I hugged her. I wanted to make sure she knew that we all make mistakes but that it's okay, especially during times like these. "Besides, now it is on their radar that we are aware of the lack of documentation, or, in my opinion, the lack of integrity."

My body stiffened as I remembered the visions I had experienced with my dad, and my mom immediately jerked away in a panic. "Are you okay honey? Are you going into another seizure? Let me go grab the nurse."

She turned to walk out of my room, and I grabbed her hand so she couldn't go any further. She turned back around, and we locked eyes. I could see her wheels turning at what it could have possibly been, but I don't think she expected what I said next.

"I saw dad."

With those three words, her face crumpled. Face in her hands she fled from my room. She had suffered too much, and the mention of Dad might have broken her. I protected my mom from a lot, but she needed to know what I saw.

A nurse walked in with my new anti-clotting medication and told me once she put it into my IV, I would need to go for a walk. She was more than happy to assist me, but I felt good enough to walk on my own, even if it was just for a short distance. I needed some time to be by myself, alone with my thoughts. I grabbed my IV stand and my cell phone, which I had been avoiding, and started strolling on my oh-so-merry way.

This was the first time I had checked my phone in a good two weeks, and it had blown up. I had 147 unread texts, 3 voicemails, and an unbelievable amount of social media notifications that I wanted nothing to do with. I looked through the texts first to see if Nathan had reached out to me. I had momentarily forgotten about him, but clearly the pit inside me had been subconsciously missing him after seeing memories of him in my dreams.

I scoured through all of my messages, and to my dismay, there were none from Nathan. So I moved on and messaged all of my friends and family back to give them updates, let them know that I was okay, and that I would hopefully be heading back to school soon. I didn't know how true my statements were, but I needed to bring comfort to those who cared enough to reach out and check up on me.

I have never been religious, but I felt the need to go and sit in the chapel, even if it was just for a sense of spirituality after the day I'd had. I walked in to see that some people had the same idea, their lit candles surrounding the room. The ambiance was warm, and it brought me peace to walk into the quiet room that seemingly existed separately from the real world.

I sat in a small wooden pew and sighed. Instead of praying, I spoke to my dad. "Daddy, I hope you know how much Will and I miss you. I would do anything to have you back in our lives. We miss your smile and laugh during the dark days, which seem to be more often than not now. I hope you're happy and able to smile down on us because we really need it."

I sat there for about 20 minutes, just letting the stress and heartache of the last few years make their way down my face. Dad was gone, and now Will might be too, regardless of the hand squeeze.

As I stood up to leave, a few more people filed into the room. I went and lit a candle for Will, in an attempt to comfort myself and in hopes that it would somehow help.

I got back up to my room, where my mother was absolutely

frantic.

"Mom, what's wrong?"

She turned around and ran to me and embraced me. "Oh honey, I thought something happened to you. No one knew where you were, and I thought of the worst case scenario." Her expression softened, reflecting the relief she was now feeling. "Now, tell me about seeing your dad. I want to know all of the details."

I told her about our conversation and how he felt so real, and that I could feel the presence of a light. I explained to her, just how I had explained to my dad, that I was a fighter and that I wasn't going to give up on this life just yet. Not when she and Will needed me. I wanted to make sure she knew I was always going to fight to be here with her, no matter what it took.

"Did you get to tell him about Will?" She asked it in a tone that told me she already knew the answer, or knew that I wouldn't want to tell him if I didn't have to.

"Unfortunately, but also fortunately, I wasn't able to because I woke up. I would have, had I gotten the chance." I continued on telling her how I explained the struggles she'd faced before becoming an even stronger woman and mother. I told her about all the memories my dad and I had talked about, and I let just a singular happy tear roll down my face.

I was glad to see a smile spread across her face as she reminisced about those memories with me. They were all great memories we had with him, and we wanted to keep them that way.

As much as we both missed him, his memory lived on through our adventures and family time. But he especially lived on through Will. He was my dad's spitting image: an almost perfect replica of him, both in looks and in personality. And the older he got, the more he reflected the nuances and body language that my father was known for.

"We are going to get some additional opinions on Will," my mom said, as if reading my mind. "I'm not giving up on him, just like your father never gave up. I know that's what Will would want."

"Did you ever figure out what happened with that? Why they didn't tell you about him squeezing my hand?"

"According to the doctor I spoke with, there was a miscommunication. But I have not been the happiest with how they've handled everything, so I'm not sure I believe that. I'm having him taken to the Barrow Neurological Institute in Arizona. It will probably be expensive, but I will do anything to make sure Will has the best chances of waking up from this."

She looked at me intently, and I could see the resolve in her face, and I was proud of her for that.

Ch 12

After what had felt like years of being in the hospital, I was finally being released. I had my new regimen of medicines to prevent me from clotting and to help with my seizures. I was so excited to go back to school. I felt like I hadn't seen everyone for so long, even though it had only been a couple of months. I had somehow caught up on my homework, with a few of my teachers cutting me a break and reducing my workload.

I was also beyond thankful to be back home in my own bed. Upon lying down, I completely knocked out for the first few hours of being home. I awoke to the smell of my mom's cooking, and I ran downstairs to check out what she was making.

"Hey, how are you feeling? Did you have a good nap?" she asked.

"Yes! Sleeping in my own bed is exactly what I needed after the last couple months." I laughed, unable to contain the joy I felt from being home. My smile quickly faded, however, as the thought of my brother still in the hospital.

"It's okay, Olivia. You're allowed to be excited about being home. You deserve that much. Let me worry about Will right now."

"You're right, I'm just so worried about him. I wish I knew that he would be okay," I said with a crack in my voice.

"I know baby, but I am the adult. Let me handle it. You have bigger things to focus on, like finishing up your senior year and applying for colleges."

I could feel the color draining from my face. With everything that had been going on as of late, I had completely forgotten about college applications. I was way more behind than I wanted to be, though I had already submitted my early admissions to the few colleges at the top of my list.

"I've been thinking I'll apply to some of the colleges in Arizona so I can be near Will through everything."

"Absolutely not, Olivia, not unless you really want to go there. I will likely be renting a place to travel out there every week so I can there with him. If he is still there once you head to college, I will move out there. But I am not going to allow you to give up on going to an Ivy League school to be with your brother. While I love you for it and your empathy, you have worked far too hard for this to just give it up. There is not much you can do for him, and I know he would never want you to give up your dream schools."

"But what about money? Ivy League schools are so expensive, and you need as much of the money you have to pay for Will's treatments. I couldn't expect you to use any of that for me with his condition."

"Olivia." She was stern this time, a serious furrow coming across her brow. "Stop, right now. You are going to one of your dream schools, and we will figure it out. I will help you find financial aid or

72

scholarships if you need it, but I am not going to let all of this go to waste. You got it?"

I was hesitant, but I knew that she wasn't going to budge. "Yes, mom. I got it. I guess I just feel guilty to think of myself in a time like this."

She understood, but she wanted me to be able to pursue my dreams. I already had so much respect for my mom for her resilience and hope. Knowing my mom was willing to sacrifice herself and her being for Will, and then ensure me that I can pursue my dreams, was almost too much. She was the mother I aspired to be in the future.

"What's for dinner?" I asked as I embraced my mom around her shoulders and gave her a kiss on the head.

"Your favorite! I made some baja tacos and got some of the raspberry iced tea that you like. And wait till you see what I got for dessert!"

She was so excited, and while it was something so little, I appreciated this moment. I knew I wasn't going to be getting a lot of them with her for the time being while she helped Will, so I soaked it in as best as I could. I squeezed her a little tighter, then gently let her go so she could finish up cooking.

"I'm going to go make sure that I don't have any homework left. Do you need any help with dinner?"

"Nope, I'll just need help with you eating some once it's done! You go ahead honey, I've got it." She turned around and smiled as she shooed me away.

I ran back upstairs and checked my school's assignment log online to see if I had missed anything. I found one assignment for my creative writing and psychology combination class that I had missed that was due at midnight. This was odd for a Saturday and likely a mistake, but I wanted to get it done so I didn't have to worry about it.

My assignment was to write a poem about a personal experience that could be understood in alternate ways depending on the perspective of the reader. The teacher said it could be anything from light-hearted to soul-searching. I felt compelled to write about my recent experiences, as they had consumed my life. There were no other parameters except a minimum of eight lines, so I got working.

I knew I wanted the poem to be from my brother's perspective because I wanted to give him a voice. As I thought about poems I had read in the past, the words flowed through me with what felt like no effort. I started scribbling on my paper, barely able to keep up with my mind. And by the end of the poem, streams of tears were pouring down my face.

Darkness caved in, when I took a final breath.

Unable to speak, unable to say goodbye, I felt myself upon the brink of death

I knew this was goodbye, a new start

But that wasn't going to heal my mother's broken heart

I wanted to give up, I wanted to let go

But instead my mother grabbed me, and now she must know

That while I was heading for the light

Something did not quite feel right

I was not ready to say goodbye

I'm not yet ready to die

I want to hold the last piece of my soul

And keep my family whole

While I was writing it from my brother's perspective, I knew a lot of what I had written was relative to how I was feeling and how I didn't want him to give up. I wanted to will him the way I willed myself when I went into a coma. But I knew that all I could do was hold onto the little optimism I had left. I grasped onto the last straws of Will's life as if mine depended on it. All I wanted in that moment was for him to feel my love wrap around him, and for him to know that I was never going to give up on him and neither was our mother.

Ch 13

Mom was still finishing up dinner when there was a knock at the door. I saw a police officer through the peephole and immediately felt distressed. I opened the door and asked how I could help them.

"Hello, is Mrs. Burke home? We need to speak to her in regards to her son's arson case."

"Uh, yes, let me grab her real quick. She's just finishing up dinner. You can have a seat on the couch while I grab her if you'd like." I turned to go to my mom then paused. I whipped back around to face the officer again. "Actually, can I see your identification real quick before I have you come in?" I had learned from a family friend's incident that you can never be too careful with people impersonating police officers.

"Yes of course," he said as he handed me his badge. I took a picture to make sure that I had a copy just in case and let him into our home.

I ran into the kitchen where my mom was putting food on our plates. She knew something was up as soon as she looked at my face. "A police officer is here. I think he's here to talk to you about Will's case."

Her face dropped.

"Is everything okay? Have you been discussing the case with

the police? Is there something I don't know?"

"Olivia, please just eat, I will fill you in later once I've spoken to him." I begrudgingly obliged and took my food outside to enjoy the cool weather and fresh air I had missed out on for the last two months. I wondered what new information the officer might have had. Had they found the suspect? Did they know what happened? I finished my dinner and headed into the kitchen to clear the dishes before my mom could get to them. I noticed her food still sitting on the dining table and put it into the oven at a low temperature so it wouldn't get cold before she was done.

I went upstairs to change into workout clothes to go for a run, or at least a brisk walk. The doctors said I could go so long as I continued taking my medication and took it easy. I figured this would be a great way to clear my mind while also giving my mom and the officer extra time and space. It was nearing 6 o'clock, but thankfully still fairly light out, so I ran downstairs to take advantage of what little light I had left.

As I grabbed the door handle, my mom came around the corner and asked me where I was going. "I need to clear my head and go on a run. I promise I will be safe." She looked concerned, but just told me to be safe and try not to be out too late.

I walked outside, popped my headphones on, and started my stretches before starting a brisk walk to make sure my body really could handle it. I didn't know where I was headed, but my legs took me where I subconsciously thought about going: the park.

It was still taped off, and most of the burnt equipment had been removed. I decided to bypass the tape because I needed to somehow connect with my brother again, and this was the closest thing I had. I sat in the middle of the playground layout, put my headphones around my neck, and just closed my eyes.

Screaming. I hear screaming. Where is that coming from…?

I opened my eyes and was surrounded by fire. "Will! Will, where are you?!" I could hear myself screaming, but it didn't sound like my voice. I look down at my hands and realize I am in Will's body. The clothes he was wearing that day that had to be cut and peeled from his burnt body were clinging to me. I looked out into the fire and saw two figures. One that seemed to look like my silhouette, and the other, while familiar, I could not make out.

"Help me! Help! It hurts, it's burning me!" Will's voice this time. Then the second silhouette came into the light, and a pit filled my stomach. It was Nathan. He looked disheveled as he pulled me from the fire, hair smelling of smoke and hands covered in soot. But none of this made sense, I wasn't at the fire, and Nathan had never mentioned that he was. Why was my imagination playing tricks on me now?

I was jolted awake by rain hitting my face. I was laying down now, which means I may have passed out. I knew I couldn't tell my mom, otherwise she wouldn't let me leave again.

I got up from the ground and left the park to go on an actual run. I was feeling great and ran about 2 miles before heading home. I rounded the corner of my street to a heavy police presence. While I was just going to continue past it, I realized that they were mostly around a familiar house: Nathan's. I ran towards the front door, but was quickly stopped by police telling me that this was an official matter, and they were trying to keep the scene contained. Thankfully Mrs. Holtz, Nathan's mom, was in the front yard and waved me over, prompting the officers to let go of me and let me proceed.

"Mrs. Holtz, what's going on? Why are all these officers here?"

"Sweetie, come inside. I need to talk to you about all of this."

My heart sank. Did something happen to Nathan? Why all of this secrecy and lack of communication with even my own mother? I walked into their home where some detectives were talking to Mr. Holtz while other investigators were searching through their home.

Mrs. Holtz took me into their office and shut the door. She moved the two chairs across from one another and then grabbed my hands in hers and told me to sit down. I reluctantly sat down and felt anxiety overwhelm me. She sat across from me and grabbed my hands again.

"What is going on? Please tell me," I begged as fear forced tears into my eyes..

"Olivia, I am going to be quite frank with you right now, because you deserve that. But Nathan is the prime suspect in your brother's case. We aren't sure why, but that's the conclusion that the police have come to. I'm so sorry this is how you're hearing this news."

I couldn't bear to be in the same room with another human soul, so I got up, took one more glance at her, and ran out of the house. I couldn't hold my sobs as I ran in the opposite direction of my house. I couldn't go home like this, not to my mom who had kept this from me. I ran until I couldn't anymore, ending up at my highschool before collapsing shortly thereafter.

Ch 14

I awoke to a flurry of chaos that included football players, teachers, and an ambulance pulling into the parking lot. I sat up rather quickly and immediately grabbed onto the closest arm to me. As I steadied myself, I took in the scene to find that many of my classmates were surrounding me. As embarrassing as it was, I couldn't think about that and focused on the water the EMT offered me. I then realized I was still grabbing the hell out of someone's arm so I let go and turned to thank them.

And there they were. Those incredible eyes that I missed staring into. Those eyes that I missed look at me in a way no other person had: Nathan. It was Nathan. I was overwhelmed. I wanted to hug him. But I also wanted to strangle him. So instead, I just sobbed. I sobbed to the point of being unable to breathe.

More chaos ensued as my mother pulled up to the scene in a police officer's vehicle. At this point, I was just accepting of the fact that the rest of my senior year was no longer going to be anything close to normal. While she tried telling EMS to take me to the hospital, I ensured them I was fine and to just allow me to go home. My mom eventually backed down, and the crowd started to disperse as I got myself up off the ground and brushed off.

I then turned back to where I had held Nathan's arm, but he was nowhere to be seen. My mom grabbed my arm and helped me to the officer's cruiser to take me home. I reluctantly got in the front seat as I frantically searched for Nathan. No such luck as my mom got in and we drove off.

We pulled up to the house within minutes, and I got out and ran upstairs. I left the light off and just collapsed on the ground as I bawled. I had locked the door as I closed it, so when my mom came banging on it, I screamed for her to leave me alone and give me some time. She quickly backed off, realizing that I was being heavily impacted by the situation and needed some space.

"Why would you do this Nathan? My brother? Of all people and things? One of two things you knew would KILL me and you did that? WHY?!" I screamed the last part in agony. I started to drift off from my sobbing, and the exhaustion wrapped itself around me like a security blanket. It was the first time I had felt safe in months..

As soon as I drifted off, I was immediately surrounded by flames again. I was myself this time, Nathan was in front of me, and a lighter and gas were on the ground between us. I bent down to pick them up and heard just a few telling splashes as the gas container slushed its contents around. I could hear Will's screaming start to fade as the smoke permeated his lungs. It hurt my soul knowing that this was potentially what he had gone through. If it was, he had suffered so much in those last moments of consciousness.

I turned back to Nathan, lighter and gas container still in hand, and screamed. "What is wrong with you?! Why would you do this?! How could you do this?!" I threw both items at him with my full power, and they slammed into his face with a force I didn't know I had.

"Olivia, please," he said as he picked the items up.

"NO!"

I jolted awake to the feeling of falling, but the security blanket tightened around me just a little more. I realized I was no longer dreaming, and someone was holding me. They must have felt my body change because they swiftly held their hand to my mouth and shushed me to calm down.

"Olivia, please, let me explain."

Nathan.

My body went rigid as he grasped my mouth a little tighter and continued holding me to try and calm me. I pushed his hand off my face and told him to let me go, or I was guaranteed to scream. I turned on my lights and turned around as he stood up to look me in the eyes. He went to grab my arms, but I shrugged him off.

"Please let me explain. If you hate me after I tell you what's going on, then so be it. But at least let me plead my case."

"How can you have a case to plead? The police are accusing you of attempted murder. And that turns into murder if my brother dies!" I realized I was shouting now, so I toned myself down to a whisper so as to not alarm my mom. "How can you explain that away, Nathan?"

His eyes were desperate. "You really think I could do something like this? You truly think I could hurt your brother like this? Or at all for that matter? Never, Olivia. Never." His voice faded away, and I could tell it broke him that I thought he was capable of this.

"Then why did you disappear? You basically left me without a trace when I needed you most. Again. You knew how much you meant to me, and you just dropped off the face of the Earth. And you expect me to believe that it had nothing to do with this situation?" I was shaking now, out of both anger and fear.

He reached a hand up to my face, and though I flinched, I let him. "Olivia, I don't even know what to say to you. I am so sorry for all of this. I am so sorry for not being there. But I'm especially sorry you felt abandoned by me in your time of need. I hope you know I didn't want that at all. I just needed to respect your mom's wishes through all of this."

"My - WHAT?!" I screamed again, not realizing until it was out of my mouth. "Shit," I said under my breath. Sure enough, my mother was at my door knocking incessantly, demanding that I let her in. Thankfully, there was plenty of room in my closet for Nathan to go into, so I shooed him in there and opened my door to my mom. Her tear-stained cheeks were all I could see.

"Honey, please talk to me. I need to know what's going on."

"I don't know mom, why don't you tell me? Why don't you fill me in fully since Mrs. Holtz is the one that had to tell me about everything."

She looked down at her feet. "I'm so sorry honey, I wanted to tell you but the police had me sign an NDA to not talk about anything regarding the case until it was public record. They wanted to be sure of things before they made anything public. I know you really cared for Nathan, but this is a horrible, awful thing he has done. I can't even fathom what his parents are thinking. They thought they raised this sweet boy but-."

"Mom, stop right there. Just because they have a warrant out, does not mean he did it. How can you automatically assume he did?

After how sweet and caring he was to me? You can really just write him off like that?" The words flew out of my mouth faster than I could realize my hypocrisy.

"What has gotten into you that you think he is innocent? What did his mother say?" My mom asked, trying to read my face as I went to respond.

"The only thing she told me is that Nathan was a suspect in this case. I didn't get any details or information beyond that. But I absolutely cannot imagine him doing something like this on accident, let alone on purpose." I was pleading a case that I didn't even know if I believed myself, but I knew my mom would be relentless if I didn't defend him.

"Okay, fine Olivia. I'm going to let this go for the night and pour myself a glass of wine. This has been enough stress for me. Are you sure you're feeling okay?"

I assured her that I felt fine and shut her out of my bedroom as I locked the door behind her. I slumped against the door as the energy drained from my body and the color drained from my face. Nathan peaked his head out of my closet door and whispered, "Is it okay to come out?" I nodded, and he carefully closed the door behind him as he approached me to grab my hands and lift me up. I reluctantly placed my hands in his, and he pulled me to the bed and helped me sit down.

My face still felt flushed, and I couldn't seem to catch my breath. It felt as if I had been punched in the gut, and I couldn't recover. Nathan started rubbing my back, and while I was still hesitant of him touching me, his touch calmed me down almost instantly. Within a few minutes, I was able to sit up straight and turn to Nathan as his hand slid off my back.

His eyes locked with mine as he spoke, "I swear. I would never do that. I happened to be by the park as the fire was ramping up, and while I was trying to save Will, I thought I saw you on the other side of the fire. I rushed over there, but you were gone, and the fire just continued to get worse. I was doing all I could to try to put some of the fire out and get to Will, but I couldn't. Then the fire truck got there, and a few minutes later, so did the ambulance."

The color rushed from my face again. So was that why I had been seeing myself in these "visions" at the park? But that didn't make any sense. I was asleep; I had taken a nap and woke up from the sirens of the ambulance rushing to the park. "I don't think you saw me, Nathan. I was asleep in bed when I woke up to the ambulance driving by."

"Then I don't know who it was, all I know is I saw someone that looked like you. Once the authorities got there, I gave my statement and watched as they finally got Will into the ambulance to go to the hospital. I wanted nothing more than to go see you first thing, but the officers on scene told me to go back home. I shouldn't have listened, I know that now," he said, his voice cracking. I could tell he was truly sorry for how things had gone, and my heart hurt for him.

"Wait, you mentioned my mom said you couldn't see me?

Why? What did she say to you?" I asked, desperately hoping for an answer I could handle.

"She said that I was not good for you, and I shouldn't be around you. She said she'd pull a restraining order against me if I tried to talk to you or contact you in any way. I just figured she was devastated by what was happening, but it seems obvious now that she must have assumed or been told I was a suspect from the get go. I just don't understand how they made that conclusion because I helped as much as I could. I stayed on scene to give a statement. I did everything right, and yet here I am, still being accused. It just doesn't make any sense."

"You need to turn yourself in. It won't look good if you hide from them. Find a good lawyer, and you'll be able to fight it," I said, unsure of how hard it would be to prove his innocence. I couldn't believe a court battle would potentially be in my future. I was ready for my life to resume to some sense of normalcy. But in this moment, it didn't feel like I could ever get there.

"I know," Nathan said, looking down at his hands. He reached out to caress mine, then looked up at me. I sunk into those eyes like a wave in the ocean. It was so comforting to see him, to feel his touch. To know that he really hadn't abandoned me and that he was being respectful of my mother's wishes.

His hand came up to wipe a tear coming down my face. His hand stayed in place as I slowly leaned towards him. He met me halfway and leaned his forehead against mine. "I love you, Olivia. I love you too much to ever hurt you. I hope you know that."

Goosebumps ran down my body as I heard those words leave his lips. It was the first time he had told me how he felt, and it felt so overwhelming. I opened my eyes and looked into his. I wished that this was coming at a better time. His hand was still on my face as I looked up at him, and he slid it down to my chin to lift it just slightly, putting my lips just an inch away from his.

"I love you Olivia, with all of my heart." My eyes welled with tears and he gently placed his lips on mine. Hesitant at first, I put my hands on his chest, gently pushing him back. He embraced my face with both of his hands, awaiting my cue to pull me in closer as he attempted to kiss me more passionately. But I quickly pulled away, breath lost, and face flushed again.

"You need to go, Nathan. You have to go. You can't be found here, or we will both be in huge trouble." I hated saying those words, but I knew I was right, and so did he.

"I know. I know," he said as he stood up reluctantly. He lifted my chin once more to look me in the eyes, and then, silently, he crawled out my window and down the tree. I could hear the leaves quietly crunch beneath his feet as he hurried back home.

I curled up on my bed as I lay my head back down to try and sleep. But all I could think about was the fact that Nathan had told me he loved me. And that I hadn't said anything back.

Ch 16

I got up the next morning for school for the first time in months. And while it felt odd, I was excited to get back into the swing of things. My mom wanted me to wait a couple more weeks, but I was dying to get back out into the world. I had been bed-ridden for far too long.

I put on my favorite outfit—a pair of black jeans and a Slytherin shirt with a black hoodie over top—before I slid into a pair of vans and headed out the door. I decided to walk to school because I knew I would need the walk back home to help clear my head. I wondered at Nathan's fate. Had he turned himself in? Had the police gone to his house to get him? I would have to stop by the Holtz residence on my way home to find out. But right now, I needed to pick up my pace and get to school.

My first step on campus felt almost surreal, but, thankfully, nobody seemed to notice my presence. Just how I liked it. I scurried up to my locker and put everything in it but my English Lit book and homework. I grabbed my notebook and stepped into my classroom just as the final bell rang. I quickly got to my seat and opened my notebook for class. Thankfully, my mom had messaged all of my teachers to not call out my presence since I didn't want additional attention cast on me. It was already going to be a rough enough transition back into real life. The last thing I wanted was the spotlight.

I went about my day until the lunch bell rang. I debated whether to head straight home or stick around to see my friends. They'd texted me throughout my time in the hospital, but I hadn't seen any of them for weeks. I headed out to our spot to find that no one was there. I waited a few minutes while looking around to see if I could spot them, but I was unable to find them. I decided to head home and take an opportunity to relax.

I walked in the door to eerie silence. Normally the alarm would be on, but my mom must have forgotten to arm it before she left that morning. I headed upstairs to my room and set my stuff down. I had the realization that I hadn't stopped by the Holtz's, but it would have to wait. I sat on my bed and thought I should partake in some self care. I grabbed a bath bomb and face mask from my bathroom and went into the master bedroom where my mom had a jet tub. I ran back to my room and grabbed my bluetooth speaker and then made myself at home in my mom's bathroom.

I blasted my favorite music that I could sing to (or scream rather) as I prepped the bathtub with hot water and my bath bomb. I sprinkled some epsom salts to add some extra healing power and slowly dipped myself into the tub.

"All I know, loving you is a LOSING GAME!" I belted out, scaring myself as I accidentally knocked the bluetooth speaker off the bathtub. I reached to grab it, and as I picked my head up, I saw a silhouette outside of the door. Chills ran down my body as I shot out of the tub and wrapped myself in a towel. Normally, I'd be terrified in a situation like this. But I knew where my dad's gun was and ran to grab it from the adjoined master closet.

It was a simple 9mm pistol, but it made me feel ten times safer than I did just a minute prior. However, instead of going out of the bathroom, I locked myself in the closet and called 911. They dispatched a few officers who were there within minutes. I could hear them knocking downstairs as I remained in the closet. I asked dispatch what I should do, and she said they'd find their own way in, and that I should remain hidden.

I remained on the line with dispatch as she told me what the officers were doing. Within a couple minutes, they had checked the perimeter for signs of entry (or of anyone for that matter), but they were unable to find anything. There were no signs of anything being open, unlocked, or even tampered with. With gun in hand, and my finger off the trigger but ready for any signs of intrusion, I ran downstairs and out of the front door as I welcomed the police officers into my house.

I stood outside, realizing I was a bit chilly, but not caring because at least I was safe now. Somehow, being in a towel outside in my front yard was not even the most embarrassing thing that had happened to me that week. I got off the phone with dispatch and just stood outside with a female officer as the rest of the officers scoped the house.

"Hi Miss, are you who called 911?" asked one of the officers as he walked out of the house.

"Yes, I did. Were you able to find whoever I saw?" I already suspected their answer, but I had to ask.

"Unfortunately not Ms. Burke. There was no sign of anyone in the house nor having been in the house. Are you certain you saw someone?" This question rubbed me the wrong way because I felt as if they didn't believe me. Why would I make this up? I had no reason to. But I answered his question as truthfully as I could, stating that I could have sworn I had, but that I was not 100% certain.

I gave my full statement to another detective and then sulked back into the house and turned on the alarm. I ensured that all of the doors and windows were locked, and then I headed upstairs to dress myself since my "self-care" time was clearly over.

I locked my bedroom and got dressed, and planned to stay in there until my mom got home. I picked up an unread book and started getting into it as a distraction. What felt like years later, though it was definitely hours, my mom came home. I heard her turn off the alarm and set her stuff down.

I ran downstairs and gave her a hug, even though I was upset with her for pushing Nathan away. I knew we would need each other more than ever for the upcoming days and challenges, and I also knew that she only did the things she did out of love, not malice. How can I be upset with that when she's my mother?

"Oh boy, are you okay Olivia? I don't remember the last time I got a greeting like that from you upon me coming home." She was asking jokingly, but as soon as she saw my face, I could tell somber thoughts were crossing through her mind.

"The police came to the house today. I had to call 911 because I saw a silhouette in your doorway when I was taking a bath."

She went as white as a ghost. "Why didn't you call me? And are you sure it wasn't Nathan?" She was still very clearly scared of him due to the allegations being thrown his way, but I assured her I didn't think he would do that.

"I'm pretty certain he would have told me it was him in the house, mom. And to that point, I don't think he did what they are accusing him of. I just absolutely do not think he is capable of those actions. And quite frankly, I am shocked you can." I was being blunt, but I needed to for my sake and for the sake of the relationship with my mom. We couldn't afford to tip-toe around issues anymore. We were both adult enough to make a decision on how to handle situations more maturely, so I decided to get that ball rolling.

"Oh Olivia, I never would have thought so if not for the evidence that they found."

My eyes blurred momentarily. What evidence was she talking about, and why had Nathan not mentioned it? "Evidence?"

"They found a lighter at the scene that had his fingerprints all over it," her tone giving away just how sad she was about the situation.

My heart felt like it dropped all the way down to my tailbone. I couldn't believe it. A lighter? He had no reason to carry one. He wasn't a smoker, and he didn't use lighters for anything else I knew of. Why would he have had that at the scene?

"I'm going to go sit outside for a bit. I need a breather." I sat down in one of our swinging chairs and just took in the weather and changing leaves as I thought about what my mom had just told me. Then my mind went to Will. Was he able to hear us? Did he know what was going on with everything? Or was he truly gone like the doctors were saying? I couldn't take it anymore, so I grabbed my phone and started reading some fanfiction to escape the realities of life.

Ch 17

A couple of hours must have passed because it was dark now. As I got ready to go inside, my mom appeared at the door. "Olivia, someone is here for you."

I couldn't imagine it was Nathan because there was little chance that my mom would let him. But who was it then? I walked into the living room and was shocked to see Nathan's mom.

"Mrs. Holtz, what are you doing here?" I asked, curious because there was no reason for her to be there.

"I wanted to check up on you from our conversation the other day. And thank you for talking to Nathan the other night. I really appreciate you making sure he didn't wait and get charges for 'evading arrest,'" she said, her fingers motioning quotation marks.

"Oh, you're welcome. I am just glad he listened to me." I couldn't help the overwhelming sinking feeling as I thought of what else that meant. "Does that mean he's in jail now?"

"He is for a few days while we get the preliminary hearing for them to set his bail. Until then, it's just a waiting game. This is going to be a long process, but hopefully the truth comes out and evidence shows that he is not the culprit. You believe him, don't you?" Her eyes glistened with tears as she asked, hoping that my answer would be yes.

I thought about it for a moment, and there was no reason not to believe Nathan. But as I thought about it, I realized I also didn't have good enough reasons to believe him either. On one hand, I couldn't imagine him ever hurting Will or vandalizing anything. On another hand, maybe it was just an accident, and he didn't want to admit it? Either way, I knew that things were going to be difficult, and until I saw evidence that solidified his guilt, I needed to proceed with "innocent until proven guilty." With that said, I also didn't want to upset my mother by saying that I believed him. But I needed to trust my gut.

"Of course I do. I was absolutely shocked at first, but after talking to him and seeing how he spoke about everything and his willingness to turn himself in, I realized that the person I am falling for would never have done something like that, especially not on purpose."

In disbelief of myself, I watched my mom's expression as I said this. It showed signs of disapproval, but she remained quiet. I wanted to reassure her that I didn't think Nathan could ever hurt Will, but I didn't feel this would be the appropriate time.

"Falling for?? Oh Olivia, that makes me happy," she said, a smile beaming on her face. "I hope that feeling sticks around long enough to prove his innocence," Mrs. Holtz said, beaming.

I couldn't believe that I said I was falling for him during the exchange. But it felt right, and, for once, I didn't question my feelings for someone. I knew I was falling for Nathan, and I knew that he was in love with me and would never do anything to hurt me. At that moment, I knew I was going to have to help the Holtz family fight like hell to prove Nathan's innocence.

"That's how I truly feel. And I will help you guys as much as I possibly can to help prove he is innocent. I just can't believe a lighter is all they have at the scene to arrest him on suspicion of this incident. Do you know if they have any other pieces, or is that the only one so far?" I was curious to know if there was any other information that I wasn't made aware of previously, since my mother seemed to be keeping things from me in order to spare me.

"No, the lighter is it, or at least so far as what we've been told. Allison, have you been told any differently?" She addressed my mother in a tone as if they were just acquaintances rather than long-term friends. My mother shook her head as she lowered it, which made me feel like she was hiding something. But I decided not to press her in the moment, and that I would just wait until Mrs. Holtz left.

"Oh okay, well I hope it remains that way. I can't imagine they would have a solid case with just that, but you never know," I said, shifting my attention to how they were feeling about everything. "How are you doing with the situation? And Mr. Holtz? I can't imagine this is easy on you guys."

"We are drained, just completely exhausted. We didn't know what to think for a while when we first found out that this was a possibility. But Nathan has assured us ten fold that he would never even think to do something like this, and we just can't imagine our young man in such a position. So now, we are just hoping that the system agrees. Anyway," she said as she stood up, "I'm going to head home to make sure my husband is doing okay since this seems to be hitting him harder emotionally. Thank you for chatting with me."

I led her to the front door, gave her a hug, then opened the door. She stepped out and about halfway down our walkway, she turned around and said, "Thank you for believing in him, Olivia. It means so much to me, and even more to him." She turned back around and disappeared into the night towards her home. I shut the door and proceeded back into the kitchen to grab myself a water and found my mom in distress.

"Mom, what's wrong?" I was confused as to what she could be so upset about.

"I can't believe I thought he could do something like this. I guess I just really wanted someone to blame and suffer the consequences for what happened to my little boy. And to think that I told him to stay away from you while you were suffering, and he fully respected it. I'm so sorry, Olivia. I keep failing as a parent. All of this is my fault. I should have been better." She was barely intelligible, and I could see her legs start to buckle from underneath her, so I ran to grab her and slowly lower her to the ground.

I leaned her against the cabinets and stood back up to grab her some cold water to calm her down. I handed her the glass, and shakily, she took it and gulped it down. I could see her body ease ever so slightly as she downed the water, and her shakes started to slow down.

"Deep breaths, mom. None of this is your fault, and I absolutely will not blame you for trying to be a good parent in protecting me. I would have done the same thing in this situation. It's hard make the right decisions as a parents sometimes, but your intent is what matters." I could tell I was not convincing her, but I hoped she would come around to the prospect.

I embraced her in a tight hug and felt the tension melt from her as she found comfort in my hug. It was nice to be able to repay back all of the times she had comforted me over the years. Though, this was not the reason I wanted to be comforting her. In fact, I didn't want us to keep facing issues that needed comforting.

"What's going on with Will? Is he being transferred?" I asked before I could keep myself from doing so. "I am so sorry, that was insensitive to bring up right now."

My mom, while pulling away from my hug, looked relieved to talk about a different subject. "He's going to be transferred in two weeks once they have a bed open up in the hospital in Arizona. The neurologist I spoke with is hopeful that they will be able to do more extensive testing to give us more, and better, answers. I am just hoping that the hand squeeze you felt was real, and not just a twitch of his body. Anyway, I'm going to go take a bath and go to bed. This has been an exhausting day of many, and I think I deserve some peace." She proceeded to stand up, grab a bottle of wine and a stemless glass, and walk upstairs.

I decided to watch TV downstairs and get caught up on some of the shows I had missed. I quickly found I was tired, and instead of going upstairs, I decided to get comfortable and fall asleep on the couch.

Ch 18

I woke up to what sounded like shattering glass. Panic set in as I jolted from the couch and grabbed the nearest object to me, which just happened to be a fire poker from the fireplace. As I wielded the weapon, I tried to stay quiet while I rounded the corners. I couldn't identify where the sound had come from, but I wanted to eliminate danger for both myself and my mom. As I approached the front door, I could see there was a hole in the glass towards the top. I turned on the light to find a large rock on the floor, surrounded by broken glass. I went to pick it up, then realized it was evidence for the police.

My mom then came running down the stairs, gun in hand. Thankfully, we were both trained in proper gun handling, so she had it pointed down towards the ground with her finger off the trigger.

"What was that?" she asked frantically. "Are you okay? Is someone in the house?"

"It was just this rock, I don't think anyone came in the house though. But I'm going to double check. Did you already call 911?"

"No, honey, I was more concerned about getting down here to make sure you were okay. I'll call them now." She grabbed her phone from her pocket while bending down to pick up the rock to inspect it, just as I was about to do moments earlier.

"Mom! Don't touch that. We don't know what's on it, and it's evidence for the police."

She jumped back and nodded in agreement as the phone dialed to emergency services. I could hear a faint "911 what's your emergency?" as I walked into the kitchen and turned on the lights. All the doors looked secure and undisturbed, so I moved up the stairs to double check everything. I went into my room and saw a letter on my bed. I had no idea where it had come from, but uneasiness overtook me as I saw it.

I grabbed the letter and tucked it in my waistband as I ran back downstairs to check on my mom. An officer was already in our doorway. This was the fastest response time I think I'd ever seen, and I was thankful for that. The police officers inspected the house, just as I had, and took the rock into evidence. My mom and I then gave our statements and let the officers out.

My mom turned to me after they had left, white as a ghost. "I don't think I want to stay here tonight, would you be okay going to a hotel for the night? The officers said they would keep someone outside, but I'd rather just avoid the situation for the night. I have some rest to catch up on, and I definitely won't be able to do that here."

I agreed and went upstairs to grab some things. Before I started packing some of my items, I grabbed the letter from my waistband and went to read it. On the front was a drawing of a place that looked awfully familiar: the park.

Dear Olivia, thank you for taking the time to read this. I know that you're hurting right now, and I wish I could help with that. Unfortunately, I know that there's not much I would be able to do for you in this. Especially since I'm in jail now."

Tears welled up in my eyes. This was a note from Nathan, but how did it get on my bed? There was no chance he could have snuck it in, and it wasn't on my bed prior to the rock going through the window. I continued reading.

You are the most beautiful girl in the world, and I wish I could be better than this... This letter sounds pretty good so far, huh Olivia? Really convincing, dontcha think?

Nausea and sweat immediately took over my senses. This letter wasn't from Nathan. I assumed this letter was from whoever had been taunting me over the last few days.

You're a downright stupid bitch, you know that? You AND your mother. Absolute wastes of space. Don't think that rock was an accident, because it certainly wasn't. Next time, that will be your head, or better yet, maybe your mother's if you tell anyone about this note. Oh, and the closer you get to figuring out who I am, the closer you get to your own demise. So just keep that in mind every time you try to figure it out. Hope you know how to sleep with one eye open.

I started to shake as I felt moisture build on my palms. How did someone know about me and Nathan? I hadn't even told my friends yet except for Emma, and the only other people who knew were our parents. Had they seen us at the park or at the movies? How else could they know? I tried to wrack my brain, but I was unable to think of any other scenarios and diverted my attention back to the letter in my hand.

The letter wasn't signed, but had:

P.S. Your brother isn't going to last much longer either, but I already started that process, didn't I? Oh, and tell the cops—I dare you. Just watch what happens if you do.

I stood to find my mom, and instantly passed out, feeling my body hit the floor before fully losing consciousness.

I woke up within a couple minutes, and thankfully, somehow, my mom hadn't heard my fall. I got myself up off the ground and ran to pack so that she wouldn't get suspicious of anything. I really needed to think hard before I involved her, because this person clearly knew who we were, where we lived, and at least part of our patterns. And they admitted to hurting Will. I was terrified for how far they would be willing and able to take things, and I knew there was no chance this ended well, no matter what decision I made.

Wait, this was potential proof to show that Nathan hadn't done it, right? I could clear his name with this letter by taking it to the police. But, what would that mean for my family? Would more people get hurt, or worse, killed? I couldn't risk that. I needed time to think, so I placed the note in the bottom of my dresser and grabbed my stuff. Before I could leave my room, something caught the corner of my eye: my window. It was unlatched, and I could have sworn it was locked just moments prior when I had originally found the letter. I reached over my desk to latch it and walked downstairs.

"I'm ready mom, are you ready to go?" She nodded, grabbed the car keys, and headed out the front door. Thankfully, the vandalizer had not damaged the car, at least not that we could see. My mom was clearly still shaken up, so I grabbed the keys from her and told her to go in the passenger seat as I was happy to drive so she could calm down.

"Where to? Did you book a room at all yet?"

"Do you mind if we stop by the hospital for a bit? I'd like to see Will, I think that would bring me at least a little bit of comfort."

I nodded, put the key in the ignition, and drove to the hospital. However, I decided to make a stop first at McDonald's to get my mom a McFlurry. They were always her favorite, and my dad would always bring one home Friday nights for her to "start her weekend off on the right foot." It was a sweet tradition, and one I regretted not continuing. I resolved myself to stop taking life for granted and to start taking better care of my mom, just as she deserved.

I ordered at the drive-thru window and pulled up to pay. As I handed the cashier my card, I turned to my mom to see her eyes full of tears, and her face stained with silent tears.

"Oh, mom, please don't cry. Everything is going to work out the way it should. I promise."

"Oh, Olivia, I can't believe I'm admitting this, but the McFlurry is what put me over the edge. I miss your father, I miss his love, I miss his comfort, I miss his support. But most of all, I miss his thoughtfulness and all of the little things he always did to ensure not only my happiness, but yours and Will's as well. I miss him dearly." And with that, she broke out into uncontrollable sobs. I frantically grabbed my card and the ice cream from the cashier and drove off, hoping to spare her my mom's breakdown.

As we drove to the hospital, I couldn't get the sunken feeling out of my gut about my window. Was my mind just playing tricks on me earlier? But then, wouldn't the police have mentioned if the latch was open? I thought about it further and relieved my anxiety with the prospect that had someone actually been in my room, the police would have seen them leave through the window and down the adjacent tree.

I pulled into the hospital lot and parked, leaning over the center console to grab my mom and give her a huge hug. She cried tears and tears, seemingly unable to catch her breath. I hated seeing her like this, but I also think she needed to let this out. She had been holding on to this pain for a few years now and had stayed strong for us through all of it. This time, it was my turn to return the favor.

As I held her tightly, the letter flashed through my mind. What would she do if she knew someone was purposefully tormenting us? That they were going out of their way to make us suffer and make our lives miserable? I couldn't have these thoughts, not now. I needed to comfort her and bring her to Will.

Ch 19

It was unpleasant to be back in the hospital. I kept my eyes peeled for the kind head nurse who always made the space feel warmer. The nurse manning the front desk wasn't sure if Will was still being monitored in the same room, or if he had been moved.. We headed to the second floor, and I grabbed my mom a blanket from the nurses' station since she was always cold in Will's room.

I got to the room just as my mom was walking out. "What's wrong?" I asked as worry consumed her face.

"He's not here. He must have been moved to a different room."

She ran down the hall to the nurses' station. I caught up to her, and we stood there impatiently. The skeleton shift was sparse, but we were desperate for information.

Eventually rounding the corner, the nurse called "How may I help you?" as she looked at both me and my mom.

"I am looking for William Burke," my mom pleaded. "He used to be in room 237B, and he doesn't seem to be in there anymore."

"Of course, ma'am," the nurse politely responded. "Let me check his chart for you and see what's going on. What is your relation to him?"

"I'm his mother. Also, why would I not have been notified of a room change? That doesn't make any sense." She tried desperately to remain polite, but a tense strain leaked through her voice.

"That's a great question. I'm actually not sure, but it could have potentially just occurred not too long ago so maybe someone hadn't gotten a chance to call yet?" The nurse said this optimistically, but her eyes shifted with unease. She attempted to keep my mom as calm as possible. The nurse shuffled through some paperwork, presumably finding Will's file. She read over the latest notes and excused herself, saying she was going to grab the doctor to ensure that the file was up-to-date.

My mother turned to me. "Something is wrong Olivia—I can sense it. She's hiding something. I know it."

"Mom, calm down," I said gently. "No need to work yourself up until you have all of the information."

"You're right... I just can't help myself. This week, or this year rather, has clearly not been going my way."

"I know, mom, but there's always a rainbow after a storm, just remember that. It may be a faint one, but it's there. And it's telling you that it will be okay. Maybe not now, but eventually." I turned my head away from her. I clung to the words that left my mouth, suppressing any other feelings as much as I could. Unknowingly to my mom, my depression had been spiraling out of control since my father passed on, but I didn't want to burden her any further than she already had been.

I leaned my head back and covered my eyes. The medical team was approaching, and I needed to remain composed. Mom was unstable, and I needed to represent our family.

"Mrs. Burke, are you available to chat with us down the hall?" It was Dr. Ferguson, Will's kind doctor. Even though his face brought familiarity, it was worrisome that he didn't simply direct us to Will.

"Of course. We wouldn't want to cause another scene, would we?" My mother asked snidely. I could tell this wasn't going to end well for anyone. I was terrified to be in the middle of it, but my mother deserved to criticize this hospital even further since they had been failing to provide the services for Will that we felt he needed.

"Mrs. Burke, please take a seat," Dr. Ferugson said as he pointed to one of the chairs in the room.

"No, thank you, I can stand just fine. Now tell me, what the fuck is going on with my son?"

This was the first time I had heard my mom cuss in years, and not because she was particularly against it, but just because she hadn't really made it a part of her vocabulary.

"I can only imagine how frustrated you are, but please, have patience with us. We are doing our best to keep up." The doctor shifted to his other leg, visibly uncomfortable with the situation. To his credit, at least he was giving whatever news we were about to receive rather than pawning it on a nurse. "With that said, Will was transferred to Barrow's today. They had a spot open up early for him in Arizona, and they helicoptered him there today. They said they called and spoke with you and got your permission."

I got chills that spread all across my limbs and down my spine. Clearly, my mom hadn't gotten that phone call. So who did? Who gave permission for my brother to be sent a state away, early, and without our knowledge?

"Excuse me? I never got a phone call. What number did they call?" My mom was eerily calm, which I'm sure was because of the sheer panic that fell across her, just as it had me.

"Let me check the notes..." he muttered then prattled off some numbers.

My mom and I looked at one another and couldn't believe our ears. That was, in fact, my mom's number. But then, how did someone else answer it? It's not like she was ever away from her phone. She had had it all day at work and was notorious for bringing it with her most of the time she got up from her desk.

"That is my number, but I absolutely swear to you that I did not answer that phone call." She began an adamant plea, but it wasn't necessary, for Dr. Ferguson knew the truth when he saw it.

He looked through the most recent notes one more time and shut the folder. "I'm going to call over there to see if he made it and to tell the hospital to put some form of security detail on him. Just to be safe. Since someone's decided that doing this was funny, whether a joke or not, we need to make sure he continues to remain safe."

Mom thanked him and combed a hand through her hair. Dr.

Ferguson nodded and headed back down the hallway. We sat in the waiting room and waited for news.

We perked up when an elderly man appeared before us. "It looks like we called and left a message for you, and our notes state that we spoke to you about thirty minutes afterward. We do have a recording available, but it is not hosted here so it will take a few hours to gain access to it," the doctor said.

"That's fine. I want access to it ASAP so I can have all the information available when I file a police report for whoever seems to be stalking us. Has Will arrived safely in Arizona? Do you guys have confirmation that he did, in fact, make it to Barrow?"

"Yes, we received confirmation that he arrived safely and was placed into a neuro room and now has security at his door. We informed them that only you and Olivia should be able to gain access unless you give explicit permission for anyone else. In the meantime, is there anything else I can do for you?"

"No," my mother said firmly. "Just get access to the recordings. I am going to be driving to Arizona tonight to see my son. And while I appreciate your help today, this hospital's incompetency is going to come to haunt it."

She turned around and headed towards the exits, with me following closely behind. She had just dropped a metaphorical mic, and I wondered as to the extent of her threat. With her dire mental state and recent exertion of energy, I knew I would be handling the wheel for most of the ride.

"Do we need to grab anything else for the drive to Arizona? Or are we set?" I asked my mom.

"I am set as long as you are." I nodded, and she went to open the driver door.

"Mom, no, I will drive us. I know you are exhausted. Please, at least take a nap and let me drive for a bit?"

"You're right—I really should get some rest. I'm also going to contact an attorney that specializes in medical negligence. That hospital cannot keep getting away with 'mistakes,'" she said, putting air quotes around it.

"I think one of my friend's parent's is an attorney, but I'm not sure what their specialty is. Do you want me to ask?"

"That would be great, Olivia. I need all the help and advice I can get."

We got into the car, I plugged the address into the GPS, and got started on our nearly twenty hour drive from Portland to Phoenix.

Ch 20

We were about 5 hours into the drive when I needed to use the restroom. I pulled into a rest stop just outside of Yreka. I stepped out to embrace the cool night air. Mom was asleep, so I locked the car and went inside the building.

Gas station bathrooms are naturally disturbing. Scanning the corners for spiders and the shadows for figures, I got in and out as fast as possible. I didn't want to come across anything unpleasant. I grabbed an energy drink after I exited the bathroom so I could spare my mom an extra few hours. I found a hallway bench near a row of windows. The moon and stars were visible in all their glory, and as I breathed it in, my phone buzzed from my back pocket. I had turned off notifications during the car ride so I wouldn't be distracted, and this influx of messages was my penance.

I glanced at my phone to find that most of the notifications were from random apps and not from actual people. I scrolled through my notifications, and noticed a text message from an unknown number. I opened it to find an audio message. While I thought it was odd, I didn't have time to listen to a 15 minute audio because we needed to get back on the road. I turned my notifications back off and walked to the car. Mom was sitting up and waiting for me when I slid into the driver's seat.

"How was your nap?" I asked, seeing that she was very much

still sleepy.

"MEH," she exasperatedly groaned and rolled over in her seat, falling back asleep.

I took off, music softly playing, all the while I wondered about the audio message and about how Nathan was doing in jail. I couldn't believe he was alone in a cell, framed for something he didn't do. I spent the drive brainstorming a way to tell police without putting my family in further danger.

It had been just over 12 hours since we began our drive, and I was starting to fatigue. My mom had slept the entire way thus far. I was glad she was finally able to get some rest, but I wasn't sure how she could be so comfortable in the car. We had just arrived in Bakersfield, so I pulled off for some breakfast and jostled her awake. It was about 10 o'clock now, so we were able to snag some McMuffins at a highway rest stop. We chowed down before our next, and thankfully final, length of our drive.

My mom switched seats with me and peeled off. We chatted a bit about how she slept and how she was feeling about driving to see Will. I hadn't realized just how tired I was and quickly started to pass out. I apologized as I pulled the blanket over my head, curled up, and let myself drift off.

Shrieking cries.. I couldn't tell where or from whom they came, but it sounded like it was a male, and it seemed like an adult. "Will, Will, can you hear me? Let me help you! Can you jump?" Then I realized, I was Will, staring into the fire as the smoke filled my lungs. I waited for my eyes to adjust and saw the muddled silhouette of a man appear before me. The crackling of the fire made the voice unrecognizable, but the somber eyes were unmistakable. Nathan. He was trying to help Will escape—at least, in *this* vision—and I hoped that this was the truth. I could see Will's hand come into sight as he reached out for Nathan. But as I looked around, there was truly no escape. If what I was seeing was true, my brother had been completely trapped.

My dream shifted. I was now reliving my memories with Nathan. From our first interaction, to the revelation at the park, to the day he came to my room before turning himself in. Reimagining these moments filled me with bliss.. I missed that feeling with him. I missed feeling important. I missed feeling loved that way. But most of all, I missed feeling whole for the first time since my father had passed. Nathan had become a loving significant other, but he had also become like a big brother for Will, and a wonderful help to my mom. He was always willing to help us, even when we told him he didn't have to.

That heavenly feeling quickly dissipated as I woke up in the parking lot of the Barrow Neurological Institute. I had completely knocked out for nearly 8 hours, and my mom, in a loving gesture, hadn't woken me. She'd made sure to grab me a salad from Wendy's along the way, which was wonderful to wake up to. I grabbed my salad and purse, and we started heading up to Will's room. We were stopped by security, so my mom grabbed her ID, and they guided us into a private suite of the hospital. We approached the security desk there and presented our ID's again, expecting to have them checked.

"Hi Mrs. Burke, you can put your ID's away," the nurse smiled at my mom then me. "Will is in room 237. Would you like me to take you there?"

"That would be great. But, out of curiosity, how do you know it is me?" my mom asked, and I was curious about that too.

"Security takes a picture of your IDs and puts them into the system for our patients that are under security. It's to ensure the safety of patients who are going through issues such as yours. We also have badges for you both so that you don't have to give us your IDs up here each time as well."

"Great," my mom said with a skeptical face. "How much extra does this cost? I want to ensure I can afford it."

"Actually, this is a government funded program to ensure patient safety. So it's at no extra cost to you. We also had this in place before, free of cost, but having the government help with the program makes us able to expand our reach."

"While that is amazing, I feel like that's fairly concerning that so many patients deal with situations like these. Don't you think?"

The nurse smiled as she looked at my mom. "I totally understand how that came across, but it's certainly not as bad as I may have implied. We just get a lot of high status patients such as celebrities since we have some of the best of the best here. But for the patients who do need it for safety, rather than privacy concerns, we are able to offer it for free so they don't have to worry about that on top of their health. Does that address your concerns?" the nurse genuinely wanted to ensure that we not only felt safe, but that we felt safe leaving Will with them.

"Yes, I definitely think so. Thank you for addressing that," my mom said and turned to me. "You feel pretty good about things?"

"Yes, definitely. I am so glad that Will seems to finally be in great hands," I said, seeing the nurse smile behind my mom.

"Great! Come this way then. I will get you your badges and over to Will's room." The nurse grabbed the two badges off the counter and walked towards the doors. She put them up to the sensor and let us in, leading the way to Will's room.

The room itself was large and beautiful, definitely fit for a celebrity. But the best part was the view. We were able to see the city and its lights while a beautiful sunset was hitting the horizon. It was definitely a sight for sore eyes, and we took it in as the nurse exited. We turned to Will's bed and grabbed a seat on each side of him, grabbing each of his hands.

We sat in silence for a minute and looked knowingly at each other. We knew the stakes. We knew the long road that was life in a hospital. This was going to be a battle, but my mom was ready to take it head on, and I was ready to back her up.

We grabbed one another with our free hands and just held tightly as we silently sobbed. A few minutes passed by, and a doctor came in to speak with us.

"I'm so sorry. I can come back later if you need me to?" Finally, a doctor with bedside manner. It had only taken Will being transferred two states away to find that.

"No, no," my mom said, wiping the tears from her eyes and her nose on her sleeve. "What information do you have for us?"

"Are you okay if I give you some realistic information and diagnoses? I just want to make sure that you understand exactly what's going on and the implications of everything. I don't want to beat around the bush because I know you have already been through so much as it is."

My mom seemed caught off guard by the question, but quickly gathered herself to respond. "Yes, absolutely. Excuse my language, but I need no bullshit right now. Tell me how it is so I can have a good understanding and get a grasp on what's going on so I can set realistic expectations. And so that we can determine a realistic treatment plan. That's all I need, and I think Olivia would agree." She turned to me, and I nodded furiously in agreement. I was ready for this all to be over, one way or another, and it couldn't be without the truth.

"Well," he took a steadying breath. "We did some workups, and it looks like Will's brain bleed has come back, likely from an aneurysm. We managed to catch it, but it had been slowly flowing for at least a couple of days, which caused pressure on his brain. Since he is in a coma, we won't know the impact of the bleed unless he wakes up. I will be honest..." he paused in the deafening silence of the room. "Things aren't looking great. However, with that said, I also don't feel it's as grim as the hospital told you in Oregon. Olivia, thank you for being such a great advocate for your brother. He deserves a chance, and he wouldn't have gotten it without you. Don't ever give that hope up. And, off the record—doctors, while they may be working in your best interest, don't always know everything. So without people like you to speak up, we can't always make an accurate evaluation." The doctor shone with honesty as he spoke to us.

It brought a smile to my face and a pressure to my chest. "Thank you for saying that. Sometimes, standing up for yourself and others is the hardest thing. It's the best thing, too, though. I am glad I did." As I finished telling him that, the letter I had found on my bed flashed across my memory. I had stood up for Will, and now I needed to stand up for Nathan. But could I? When the stakes were so high? What if his family would also be in danger if I did? "Fuck," I mumbled out loud, unable to keep it from slipping out.

The doctor flashed his eyes in sympathy for what he thought was a comment on Will's condition. He patted me on the shoulder in an attempt at comfort before turning to my mom.

"Mrs. Burke, how would you like to move forward with your son's case? To fill you in fully, we ran some bloodwork, took scans of his head and lungs, and did an overall inspection of his body. We're still waiting on the results, but is there anything else you'd like us to run in the meantime?"

My mom thought about it for a moment and shook her head. "No, not that I can think of right now. However, why did he have an aneurysm? Can smoke cause that?"

"Unfortunately, smoke damage can cause anything from a stroke to hemorrhaging in the brain, so it's hard to discern the exact cause. But chances are, with all of the trauma he's been through and the lack of resources at the hospital, it could have just been a small bleed from the get-go that never stopped and got bigger as time went on. We are very lucky that this wasn't worse."

Chills traveled down my body. Not because it could be worse, but because the sick human responsible was still roaming the world. A violent person with the capacity for harming children ran free. We *were* lucky to be at this hospital—had we just kept Will in Oregon, we likely would have lost him. These last few months had been a blur, and we weren't even out of the thick of it yet.

"I'm very glad to know all of that information Dr....?" My mom inquired as we both realized he hadn't identified himself when he first entered the room.

"Dr. Larson. I apologize that I didn't introduce myself."

"Oh no, that's totally okay," she responded. "I normally would have asked, but I guess I got caught up in the moment. Thank you again. I really appreciate all of this. Our experience here has already been miles better than at the previous hospital."

Dr. Larson looked up from the notes he had been reading off of and smiled. "Of course, I am happy to help where I can and make this process as easy as possible for you. I'm going to head out for the night, but if you need anything from me or any other doctors, please let the nurses know, and they will get in contact with me. Your son's brain and lung capacity is on constant monitoring now, so we will know immediately if he swings either way."

With his absence, we were left with still silence and loud thoughts. We sat in that silence for about twenty minutes before I grabbed my salad and ate at the small table in Will's room. The view of the night sky and lights was beautiful but very different from home. I wasn't used to so much city light pollution. We were from Portland but lived on the outskirts of town away from the hubbub.

"Olivia, I'm going to go down to grab myself something to eat. Do you need anything?"

"No, I'm good. Thanks though mom. I really appreciate it," I smiled at her before turning back to my food and view. I heard the door close behind me and took a deep breath. The first one I had fully inhaled since leaving Oregon. Surprisingly, Will's room had a window I could open to let in all the fresh, cool air. I looked out to the city, awash in the clinical light behind me, and thought about Will.

Ch 21

A nurse walked into the room, the cart wheeling in front of her. "Oh hello! I'm so sorry. I didn't realize anyone was in here. Are you okay if I do my nightly rounds with William?"

"Not at all." I said, thrown off by her use of Will's full name. "What kind of medicines are you going to be giving him?" I had started tracking both of our medications in Oregon and wanted to continue.

"It's his propofol as well as some other medications to regulate his sugars and help with promoting healing within his brain."

"Propofol? Is that what is keeping him in his coma?" All I knew about the drug was that Michael Jackson had died from it, but I did not know that it was used in situations like these.

"Yes ma'am, we have to give him a few doses each day to ensure that his brain really does get to heal," she said kindly, with a soothing tone to her voice.

I sat back and watched her administer the medications and do her charting to show the times and dosages that she had done so. "I'm Olivia, by the way," I said as I reached my hand out to hers.

"I'm Ashley. It's great to meet you. I assume you are Will's sister?" she inquired.

"Yes, and my mom is here as well, but she went down to grab

herself some food to eat. It's been a long day for us driving from Oregon."

"Oh, Oregon?! That's where my family is from. The Portland area. I love it there. I really miss it. My sister and I moved out here not too long ago. I moved for this job opportunity while she is working on her undergraduate degree and living with me to save money. We, unfortunately, haven't been able to go back," her face dropped in sadness, and I could only assume she was thinking of the family that they had left behind.

"That's refreshing, I feel like no one is from out there! What part of Oregon?"

She turned back towards Will to inspect his IV. "I'm from a small town called Hillsboro. It's northeast of Portland."

My mom walked in and heard this, and she looked up from her phone. Suddenly, her face flushed white as if she had seen a ghost. But she didn't acknowledge anything and just said hello to Ashley and sat down in the seat across from me.

"Hello! It's so great to meet you," the nurse said, outstretching her hand. How about yourself Olivia? What area are you guys from?"

"Actually, we are from the Rock Creek area, so not too far from your hometown," I responded. Shortly following, my mom kicked my foot in order to tell me to stop talking.

"Oh wow, what a small world!" Ashley exclaimed with a smile. "I'll be back in a couple hours to check in on Will. Do either of you need anything in the meantime?"

I looked at my mom, who shook her head, and said, "No, I think we are good for now. Thanks for the offer."

"Of course! Just ring the nurse's button if you need anything." Her shoes padded softly as she left the room.

"What was that about?" I asked as I turned to my mom.

"Nothing, please don't worry about it."

Normally, I would have let something like this go, but her tone pushed me on. "Mom, tell me right now what the hell is going on."

She sighed, clearly not thrilled about having to tell me what was happening. But I needed to know, especially with everything going on.

"She is the daughter of old friends. We had a falling out a few years ago, and I was just shocked to see her here," my mom said nonchalantly. I knew that couldn't be the reason she reacted the way she did. So I kept prying.

"And?" I asked.

"We kept this a secret from you because we didn't want you stressing out about this. Will used to be friends with their son, Jason, Ashley's brother. He used to bully the crap out of Will for being on the smaller side and stuff like that. And then their mom, Jennifer, used to work with your father for the longest time. She claimed that they were having an affair, but your father assured me that was absolutely not true and there was no evidence that they were. She was also fired not too long after he passed due to drug and alcohol abuse and was sent to rehab. Not sure what has happened to her since, but I know that her and her husband's marriage fell apart after that. That family really did a lot of effed up things to ours. I really hope Ashley is different from them." I could tell my mom was in pain telling me about this. I'm sure partly due to the fact that she was opening up old wounds, but also the fact that she had kept it from me all this time.

"I would have defended Will. You know that right? I would have protected him had you let me know." I was irrationally angry that they hadn't told me sooner. I could have saved him from pain.. I had always been there for him, and I had even been bullied for wanting to protect him. We didn't have the typical brother-sister relationship. We had always been incredibly close, even with our age gap. I loved him from the start, and I never allowed people to treat him less than what he was.

"I know honey, and I'm so sorry. It was just too much to handle, even for us as adults. The last thing I needed was you worrying about him and defending him. You were just a child, too. I couldn't pile things onto you. It was my job as a parent to handle it." She had been looking down the entire discussion, and her obvious sense of regret made me reach for her.

"Mom, please don't cry. I don't want you to feel bad. I just feel sad that I wasn't able to help defend him in those moments. I just want you to know that I would do absolutely anything for either you or Will. You know that right?" She nodded, shaking softly. I grabbed her tighter as her body trembled.

"I am just so tired Olivia. I am tired of dealing with sadness and grief. I am tired of missing your father. I'm just tired." Her body continued to tremble with emotion. She needed a reprieve.

"I'm here to help, in any way I can. You know that, right mom? Please tell me you know that," I pleaded, wanting to make sure my mom knew how much everything she had done meant to both me and Will.

She just nodded into my chest and continued her silent sobs. I grabbed her under the arms and pulled her to the couch in the room. I grabbed a pillow and sat down, placing the pillow on my lap while simultaneously lifting her head as I gently helped her rest her head in my lap. I started stroking her hair and rubbing her back, and I could feel the sobs slowly start to fade as she drifted off into a restless sleep.

I grabbed my phone out of my pocket to scroll through some videos as she slept. I had it nearly on mute, but was able to hear enough to get by. After scrolling for about twenty minutes, I contorted myself around her on the couch. Then I remembered the audio recording I had been sent earlier. I still hadn't listened to it yet. I grabbed my phone and went into my messages. There it was. The message thread labeled it from an unknown recipient.

I started playing the recording. Dead silence. I turned my volume up, and still nothing. What? Why was it not playing anything? Did someone really send me a 15 minute audio clip with no audio?

"AHHH HELP ME!" screamed my phone. Nearly dropping it, I scrambled to turn the volume back down to save my mom from the piercing cry.

"What the fuck," I whispered under my breath. I had no idea what I had just heard and wasn't sure I wanted to find out. I tentatively listened on.

"Please, please help me. I'm stuck up here!"

Another voice.

"Let me help you! Can you jump? I can catch you!"

"I don't think so. It's too far! There's too much smoke!"

Two male voices were calling back and forth. Both tugged at my heart for different reasons. It sounded like Will and Nathan—just like the dreams I kept having.

"Will, you're going to need to jump. I can't help you otherwise. The fire is too dense," Nathan's desperate voice came over the audio recording. How did this person record this? Were they there the whole time? "Firetrucks are coming, but I don't know how much time you have with the smoke around you. Please, Will, please jump," the desperation quickly became heavy and palpable through the phone.

Coughs ensued over the audio, with a small "Help me. Please help me!" muffled through the cracking of the fire. Quiet sobs quickly dwindled out, as did the coughs. Will must have lost consciousness at this point, because I could only hear Nathan's screaming over the raging fire.

The faint sound of emergency vehicles appeared but quickly faded and were replaced with running and heavy breathing. Then

127

silence. I had just listened to what was potentially Will's last moments on audio, and I still had no idea who was doing this to us. I wanted to bring justice to my brother, whether he pulled through or not. The person who recorded this audio would be the answer.

I started to probe into reverse searching the audio and understanding the data in the audio file. I wasn't able to find as much information as I wanted, but it was a start. I set my phone down and laid my arm on the back of the couch to use as a pillow while I allowed my mom to continue sleeping comfortably on my lap.

Ch 22

The next couple days went by in a flash, and my mom bought me a plane ticket to go back home because I needed to finish the semester out. I also needed to send out finalized supplemental material for the schools I had been conditionally accepted to. We had stayed in the hotel room while discussing logistics, and I started packing my stuff. Once I was finished, my mom and I drove over to the hospital.

As we arrived, my mom parked at the front entrance and turned to me. "Olivia, I'm going to go run some errands real quick. I will be back in about an hour to take you to the airport."

"Okay. Thank you for the heads up. I'll just talk to Will so he still remembers me when he wakes up," I said humorously. My slight smile turned into a subtle smirk because that was Will's way of thinking, and he would have been proud of me for keeping a positive mindset. My mom smiled back at me as I exited the car.

I quickly made my way into the private sector and into Will's room. I pushed the nearest chair to Will's bed. I grabbed his hand in mine and gently rubbed the top of it with my thumb. I missed my little brother, and I was sad that he had already missed so many months of his childhood. Clinging to hope, I remembered that this span of time would seem incredibly small in the grand scheme of things.

I talked to Will for about 20 minutes and reminded him of all of the beautiful memories we had had over the years. Even our tragic memories had beautiful moments marked by sibling love and support. I reminded him that we were resilient and told him of how the Burke family doesn't give up and that he could get through this. Unfortunately, he showed no signs of acknowledgment. No hand squeezes, no fluttering eyelids, not even a twitch.

My phone buzzed. It was my mom letting me know that she would be back in about 20 minutes. I was ready, but double checked that I hadn't missed any of my stuff and then sat back down next to Will. I pulled out my phone to play some music for him, but, for some reason, my phone was open to the audio recording I had been sent. Will and Nathan's voices carried from the speaker, but I quickly exited the app because I didn't want it to be a negative trigger for Will, coma or not.

I looked up at Will to admire the innocence in his face, but found myself looking eye to eye with him. I jumped back, startled by his eye contact. I shut mine tightly and reopened them, but sure enough, his were still open.

"Will? Will you're awake?" There was no response. Then suddenly, his eyes turned towards me and his mouth opened. I couldn't understand what he was saying. His lips moved and a faint and garbled sound emerged.

"What? Will, I can't understand you," I said as I leaned in.

Then, clear as day, Will said, "Get them."

"Who? Get who Will? The people who hurt you? Who was it?

Do you know?" Desperation clung to my voice like a wet newspaper on the sidewalk. "Please tell me, Will. I can't get them if I don't know who it is."

"J-j-j-j-j," Will was attempting to speak, but couldn't get the words out. "Sor-r-r-ry," he said as his eyes closed and his body went limp again.

"No!" I cried out. "Will! Come back! Please come back," I sobbed, devastated that I only had a moment with my brother. I laid my head on his side and sobbed into the blankets, feeling at a loss.

I was brought back to reality when my phone started buzzing. It was my mom, so I quickly picked up. "Hello?"

"Olivia, where are you? I texted you 5 minutes ago that I was down here and haven't heard back. You need to get down here, or you're not going to make your flight." She sounded upset, but more concerned than anything.

"I'm sorry, mom," I rasped. "I'll be down in a minute." I knew I couldn't tell my mom about Will just yet. She didn't even know the extent of the other incidents, and I wasn't about to tell her right before I hopped on a flight back home. We hung up the phone, and I ran into the bathroom to splash some cold water on my face to try and minimize the appearance of my crying. I walked out of the bathroom and collected my purse and thoughts. The door swung open and in walked one of the nurses with a tray of medication.

"Oh, hello! I'm Nurse Melissa." She reached her hand out to mine.

"I'm Olivia," I said as I shook it back. "I do apologize, though, I am heading out and have to make a flight."

"Oh, no worries. I'm just here to give William some of his medications. I hope you have a safe flight wherever you are going," Melissa said as she smiled at me. Her genuine smile gave me a pang of guilt for not telling her about Will. I knew I didn't have time for explanations, and my mom would kill me if I missed my flight. I was also hesitant to trust the nursing staff after the negligence of the previous hospital.

I half-assed smiled back and left the hospital room. I knew my mom was already going to be upset with me, and this was just delaying the inevitable. Thankfully, the airport was nearby and I didn't need to check any bags.

My mom had pulled up to the curb outside the visitor reception area. I opened the passenger door, sat down, and put my backpack by my feet.

"What took you so long? And why is your face red?" my mom asked, concern spreading across her face.

"Oh, I just ran down the stairs to get here," I lied. I couldn't tell her the truth of what had just happened. I neither wanted to give her hope nor worry her further, at least not just yet. I needed to see what I could figure out on my own without adding additional burden to my mom.

"Oh, okay," a sweep of relief crossed her face. She shifted into drive and peeled out towards the airport. I marveled at the airport's size as we approached—the airport back home only had a tiny terminal with two runway strips. Phoenix Sky Harbor truly was a looming, world-class structure that put others to shame.

I got out of the car, as did my mom, and I gave her one last hug. She had told me in the car that she wasn't going to be coming home for at least a month. Her job was allowing her to work from home however much she needed. They were even considering making her fully remote so she didn't have to worry about going into the office. They had told her she was far too valuable of an asset to lose, so they would do whatever they could to make things as easy as possible for her. I reassured her that whatever she needed to do was fine and that I'd figure things out. She thanked me, gave me a kiss on the cheek and got back in the car to pull away.

I turned around, facing the airport doors. I released a deep sigh.

I got into the security line and set my stuff on the conveyor. I pulled out my laptop, took off my shoes, and made sure I took off my watch so as to not set off the metal detectors. I got through security and decided to figure out where my gate was so I could venture nearby. Thankfully, it was about a 2 minutes walk from where I was, so I was able to do some shopping. As I grabbed myself a drink, snack, and magazine to read while I waited, I couldn't help but think about my dad and how much I missed him. He loved traveling, which was limited the last few years of his life. I walked into a different store that had trinkets and found a pyrite necklace accented with some malachite. Those were my dad's two favorite stones, so I decided to get it for myself. I also knew that these crystals promoted protection and healing, and I could use a lot of that right now.

I started heading back towards the gate and grabbed a seat right by where the seating lines form. It seemed to be a very slow day at the airport, which I was very thankful for. It allowed me to take some time and put together materials for my college applications.

The attendant's voice came over the speaker calling for the first boarding groups. I grabbed my ticket to check my own group and seat to find that my mom had purchased me a first class ticket. While it wasn't too long of a flight, I was grateful that I would have more breathing and leg room.

I popped my headphones over my head with just enough of my right ear peaking out that I could hear the announcements over the speaker. I was busy reading an article about dating, which felt completely irrelevant to me, when I felt someone sit two seats over. I glanced to my right to find a fairly attractive guy looking at me. We made brief eye contact, and I quickly went back to my article.

"Hello, passengers for flight 2386, service to Portland. We are now pre-boarding. For anyone who needs extra time, assistance, or has small children, or is in the military, you are welcome to start boarding now."

A small wave of people got up to line up, though they were not partaking in pre-boarding. After a few minutes had passed and only a couple of people had boarded, the announcer came on the speaker again. "Alright Flight 2386, all first class seats may board at this time."

I stood up and walked to the stand, noticing that the guy who had been sitting by me was closely behind. I was in the second row of three next to the window, so I quickly placed my carry-on above my seat and scooted into my seat. I immediately buckled and went to put my headphones fully on in order to block out the airplane. However, I was unable to get the headphones over my ears before the mystery guy sat next to me.

This guy looked to be about 6'2" (though, admittedly, my estimates on heights were not usually great). He had chocolate brown hair, bright green eyes, and a very athletic build. He almost looked like a combination between Ian Somerhalder and Jesse Metcalfe, which brought back the nostalgia of my middle school days of watching, and admittedly drooling over, these guys I never thought I'd have a chance with.

We made eye contact again, and neither of us broke it as he reached his hand out. "Hi, I'm Brent."

I inspected his hand for a moment then tried reading his face to determine if he had any motives. I wasn't able to determine much, but I didn't immediately get any negative gut feelings. I'd learn not to trust strangers someday, but I still held onto the hope of genuine kindness.

"I'm Olivia, nice to meet you."

We went on to have small talk about our lives and discovered we liked the same few restaurants in Portland. He was also a senior at a neighboring school about 10 minutes away and was waiting on acceptance letters from universities.

"Oh really? Like where? Do you know what you want to study?" I asked, genuinely curious what another small-town person was looking to do with their future.

"I'm going to go to law school. I'm almost done with my undergraduate degree with all the credits I've been taking during my dual enrollment program. Wherever I end up, it should only take two semesters before I can take the LSATs and transition into their law program. My hopes are Yale or Harvard, but Georgetown has a great law program too. What about you? Any idea of what you'd like to do or where you'd like to go?" He also seemed genuine in his questioning, and it forced me to really think about it. I hadn't done much of that with Will's condition, and I was approaching the normal application deadline. At least I was able to submit early acceptance applications to the same schools, Yale and Harvard.

"Weirdly enough, I, too, would love to go to either Yale or Harvard. They are the only ones I have applied to so far due to some family stuff, and I'm not sure I'll be able to submit anymore in time. How many applications have you submitted so far?" I wanted to know just what I was getting myself into since it had been a while since my last application.

"It hasn't been too bad. I am sure you know that Yale and Harvard are tough since you applied, but I also sent in my essays for Stanford and Columbia. Dad insisted that I submit scholarship essays to get extra writing practice in before college. I'm just hoping I don't get selected to win so that someone who really does need it, gets it," he looked me in the eyes again as a slight smile spread across his face.

"Wow, that's really nice of you. I hope you don't win, but that they still let you know that you wrote an incredible essay still. I feel like that would be a good consolation prize. What do your parents do for work?" I asked.

"Oh, my dad is an attorney. My mom passed away two years ago in a car accident, so it's just us. But he makes plenty enough to cover my tuition and boarding, so there's no point in me taking money from someone that really, truly needs it."

This time, it was my turn to smile. He was restoring a little bit of lost faith in humanity with what he was telling me. However, I was still curious as to why he had spoken to me so openly and been so friendly.

"I have a random question. Not that I'm complaining by any means, but is there a reason you started talking to me? I just find that people don't tend to talk to one another anymore, so it's interesting to see someone do that," I said, nervous about his reply.

"Honestly? I thought you were attractive, and then I saw *Beartown* sticking out of your bag and knew you were a girl of taste, for both the book and hockey," he revealed with a blush. His face, ears, and neck had turned crimson red, as I felt mine start to flush.

"A fellow hockey fan, eh? My dad got me into it, and I immediately fell in love and haven't fallen out since," I smiled at that fond memory as I remembered the day my dad introduced me to hockey. It was the first game of the season, and we were in Arizona. The Arizona Coyotes played the Washington Capitals that night and won 5-2 in front of their home crowd. The energy was electric, and I loved every second of the sport. I even started playing it at one point and wasn't too shabby. That was, until some kid decided to try to take my head off and concuss me. After that, I decided that soccer and golf were my sports and that I should avoid high risk situations like that.

"That's amazing. My mom got me into hockey. She was a fiery Russian who couldn't go without it. She was actually driving home from Vancouver after she had watched a couple games there and got into her accident. She was killed by a drunk driver who fled the scene and hasn't been seen since." He looked up to see my face, which was rightfully full of concern. "Oh my goodness, what a way for me to kill the mood. I am so sorry," he apologized to me.

"Don't you dare apologize," I said emphatically. "I have no problem listening to you. It's sad of me to say, but I'm thankful to hear that I'm not the only one going through hard times lately. Maybe one day I'll tell you of my sorrows." I thought about that for a second then said, "Well, well, well, now look who is being dramatic." I laughed, and it was the first time I had in days. Brent laughed softly with me, and it felt really good.

"Whatever makes you comfortable," Brent said. "I don't want you to feel like you have to say anything, so please let me know if I make you uncomfortable."

I nodded, and we went back to small talk. I didn't want to give him too many details because I was still very weary of what was going on with my own family. I was honestly terrified of giving any person, let alone the wrong person, any leverage at all. It was sad that I had to think this way, but I would do anything to protect my family at this point.

At about the halfway point of the flight, the conversation faded, and I put my headphones on so I could read my magazine. I felt myself drifting off, so I grabbed my neck pillow and adjusted myself to be comfortable. I started to fade, ready for the power nap I was about to have. I fell asleep and all was normal. Thankfully, I didn't have any dreams. I really didn't want to explain that away to Brent.

I woke up to the cabin *ding* telling us that we were landing shortly. I had slid over during my nap, and my head was resting on Brent's shoulder. I quickly lifted my head up off of him, and turned to make eye contact.

"I am so sorry," I said. "I don't normally fall over like that. I guess I was more exhausted than I realized."

He looked at me and seemed concerned. "Oh no, don't worry about it. I'm just glad I could be comfortable for you when you were taking a nap," he laughed. "Do you feel rested?"

"I do, thanks. I'm still sorry I invaded your space," I said as I gathered my things. Then a wave of stress passed over me. My mom had the car. What was I supposed to do? Where was I supposed to go? I had no way of getting anywhere, and I knew my mom couldn't afford a bunch of Uber rides for me if I needed it. I made a plan to message Emma, who had a similar schedule to mine, as soon as we landed.

"You okay?" Brent asked, noting my furrowed brow.

"Oh yeah, I just have to figure out some things once I get back home. No biggie though," I smiled in hopes of taking him away from the subject. Thankfully, it worked and we went back to silence.

I grabbed my headphones and started blasting some Ludovico Einaudi. It had always helped me enter a creative space, and I used it in this moment to think about what my life might have been had my father made it through his diagnosis and had Will never suffered from the flames. We had always been a close-knit family, something I recognized and appreciated. No matter how upset with one another we were, we always came back at the end of the day to dinner with apologies and love. We would never go to bed angry. That was something my parents preached, even before my dad's diagnosis. They told us it was because you never knew when it may be someone's last breath.

Then Nathan popped into my head. I wondered why I hadn't thought of him all day. I realized it was difficult to concentrate on one thing at a time, let alone balance my love life, if I was being honest. All I could think about was him alone in his cold cell, wishing I could get him out, hoping that his innocence eventually would. I couldn't trust the justice system to do the right thing by him, but I also couldn't trust that the person threatening me was just full of hot air. I couldn't take any more risks because I didn't want to put my life, or worse, any of my loved ones' lives, in danger anymore. If it came down to it, I would sacrifice myself in any capacity to ensure the safety of all those I loved.

Yet again, I recalled my gentle and kind memories of him. But this time, it was outshined by the audio file I had listened to. As these wonderful memories crossed my mind, I was also hearing Will scream for his life and Nathan screaming to help him. Reliving that made my soul heavy, and I could feel tears start to swell behind my closed eyes. I turned towards the window and looked outside so I could let the tears fall freely. It was dark now, and I was ready to be home.

A sinking feeling was all I could register in that moment. I couldn't go home. It wasn't safe with my mom there, let alone with her gone. I decided messaging the Holtz family would be my best bet. Mrs. Holtz seemed to like me, and she was encouraging of Nathan turning himself in. But they were sure to be on edge with everything going on, which meant I had no idea how they would respond.

I subtly wiped my eyes as I saw us approaching the runway. My tray table was already up, so I bent over to make sure that my backpack was zipped up so I could make a quick exit. I really hated holding up lines, especially in airplanes since everyone is typically ready to be home at that point.

I felt a tap on my shoulder and turned to see Brent looking intently at me. I pulled my headphones down the back of my head and to my neck. "What's up?" I asked.

"Please let me know if this is too forward, but I'm hoping I could take you out on a date some time? I really enjoyed our conversations and would love to have more," Brent asked. He was confident, but didn't exude cockiness, which I appreciated.

I thought about his offer, but even without the Nathan drama, I couldn't handle having an additional person to focus time and energy on. He could have been a nice distraction, but my feelings for Nathan were at the forefront of my mind. Adding another guy into that mix was just too much with everything else I was trying to manage. I could feel my mental health declining over the last few weeks, and I couldn't imagine sparing energy for anyone else.

"I really do appreciate the offer. But, because of everything going on in my life, I don't think it would be fair of me to expect someone to sit around waiting for me to plan a date that likely isn't going to happen any time soon," I responded, internally cringing because I was scared he would lash out at me like most guys I had encountered.

"Oh, I totally get it. I just knew if I didn't shoot my shot, I would be kicking myself." He seemed bashful, and I felt bad because I hated rejecting people. He smiled and asked, "Do you need an extra friend in your life? I could definitely use someone that understands the grief of losing a parent around."

This is the kind of person I would make friends with on a normal basis, so I was compelled to agree. "Yes, I would really like that. It's hard talking about a subject that most people don't understand. It's like hitting my head against a brick wall. And it's nothing against them, it's just really difficult to vent about it in those moments. So I just keep quiet and let it bottle up, which is no good either," a slight chuckle escaped my throat at that prospect. I was a pro at laughing about trauma and seemed to be doing it more and more often.

"Great!" he exclaimed, then ducked and shrugged out of embarrassment. "Whoops, I didn't mean to be that loud or enthusiastic. Just a little excited." He tried to turn and hide his obvious embarrassment. He grabbed his phone and handed it to me. "You okay to put your number in my phone?"

"Yeah, absolutely." I smiled genuinely. I didn't want him to be embarrassed and appreciated his respectful reply.. It was a nice change of pace. In the past, I had found myself being verbally assaulted by guys if I rejected them, and no one deserved that.

We pulled up to the gate as I handed Brent's phone back to him. We filed off the plane together and headed the same direction towards baggage claim and rideshare pickup.

"It was nice to meet you, Olivia. I look forward to having you around." Brent smiled, his perfectly, pearly whites fully showing for the first time since we had started talking. He had a contagious smile, and I could feel the corners of my mouth turn upward into a sizable grin.

"You too, Brent." I turned to go to the rideshare area, but something stopped me from going forward. I turned around, and he was already heading towards the carousel his luggage would be on. "Wait! Brent! Let me keep you company until you get your luggage."

I figured it couldn't hurt to spend a few more minutes with my new friend.

He turned around, still grinning ear to ear. "I'd love that."

We stood at the end of the carousel to avoid the crowd of passengers clamoring for bags.

"Actually, can you watch my carry-on? I really need to use the restroom real quick before my drive home," Brent asked as he glanced around to find a restroom.

"Oh yeah, absolutely. Have at it," I responded. Brent thanked me and ran off to the restroom. I took advantage of this time to look him up on social media and google search both his and his dad's name. Sure enough, he was telling the truth. Not only was his dad one of the best attorneys in the state, but Brent himself was an all-state athlete with scholarship offers up the wazoo. "Impressive," I whispered under my breath.

"What is?" Brent's voice came from behind me, causing me to jump.

"Oh, I was just watching some sports clips of people doing cool tricks on Instagram," I said, desperate to not reveal the truth to Brent and make him uncomfortable.

"Oh nice! I love watching those kinds of clips. They make me realize I could always be better," he said. Meanwhile, all of the athletic rewards and scholarships he had earned over the last few years flashed through my mind.

"Yeah, me too!" I responded, realizing I hadn't told him much about my personal life.

"You play sports? That's awesome! Which ones?" he inquired.

"Oh boy, I just opened a can of worms," I thought to myself. I had kept myself pretty detached from the conversation and couldn't believe that this was the moment I accidentally slipped.

"Oh, I play golf and soccer. I obviously also used to play hockey, but there aren't a lot of leagues around here, so that was more of a hobby," I answered, hesitantly.

"That's amazing! Glad I was able to pry a small amount of your life out of you." I could tell he was genuinely curious about me but had been respecting my boundaries since I hadn't been volunteering information on my own. "Hey, I probably know what your answer is going to be, but do you need a ride home? I'd be happy to give you one since you don't live too far."

While I normally wouldn't accept a ride from a virtual stranger (I had listened to far too much Crime Junkie Podcast), I felt very comfortable around Brent. I knew his situation and that he was being honest with everything he had told me, which made me feel safe around him. So I answered in a way I never thought I would. "Yes, actually, that would be really nice. I just need to make a quick phone call." I needed to call the Holtz family to see if I would be able to stay with them. I would stay at home if I had to, but I definitely preferred the prospect of being around other people and not alone in a home that I had been terrorized in.

"Great! The bags are going to be up any minute now, so we will be able to leave once you finish," he smiled again, that brilliant smile. Something about it felt familiar, like home. Images of Nathan started flashing in my mind, and I couldn't help but feel a pang of guilt even though I wasn't doing anything wrong. And come to think of it, Nathan had never even officially asked me to be his girlfriend. There hadn't been time to discuss a relationship, if that was even something he wanted.

I called the Holtz's but did not get an answer. I decided to call my friend Emma, who was thankfully up, and asked if it would be okay if I came and spent the night. Her parents knew about the situation I was going through and that my mom would be in Arizona for some time. I had forgotten they had offered their spare bedroom or casita to my mom for me to use while she was gone. Emma confirmed that was absolutely still the case and that she would be up to greet me when I got there. I thanked her, hung up the phone, and walked back to Brent.

"I am all set," I said, eyeing his newly obtained bag. "You good to go?"

"Yep! I'm in the parking garage on the second floor, so I'm pretty close." He not only grabbed his suitcase, but mine as well, and started trekking towards the garage.

"You don't have to do that, silly!" I said as I reached my hand forward, motioning to grab the bag back from him.

"Yes I do! This is polite and gentlemanly," he teased as he picked up the pace, quickly putting a gap between us.

"Fine! Just don't leave me behind because that's not very gentlemanly," I said with a smile. He turned around and winked, and suddenly my abdomen was filled with butterflies. I took a deep breath in to calm myself down, not understanding why I was suddenly feeling like this. The butterflies quickly faded as I caught up to Brent while he was getting on to the elevator. "Jeez, Speedy Gonzales. What's the rush?!"

"Just gotta keep you on your toes, m'lady," he said as he motioned a "tip of the hat."

"This year has kept me plenty on my toes," I said with an eye roll. "So I'm good without that for a little bit."

Brent looked at me to read my face, and when he realized I was being sarcastic, he smiled and pushed the button for the second floor. We rode up in silence, and I got lost in my thoughts again, this time about my mom and how she was doing. As we stepped off the elevator, I decided to call her and let her know that I was on my way to Emma's.

"Oh, that's great honey. I am going to bed. Text me when you get there so I know you're safe. Can you also share your location in case you forget to message me please?" My mother knew me well and my tendencies to forget to text her, or anyone for that matter. I agreed and told her I loved her, then hung up the phone just in time to get to Brent's vehicle.

I'm not sure what I was expecting him to drive, but it certainly wasn't the car I saw in front of me. It was a brand new Tesla that still had the new car smell. "Wow, this is a really nice car," I said, trying not to gawk at it.

"I know, I know. This is such a spoiled rich kid's car. But my dad mostly got it for me because of the safety ratings." He looked up at me, clearly embarrassed about the vehicle. I wondered if he had been taunted previously. But I figured this car was necessary for his dad to feel comfortable about Brent driving around. He had lost his wife to a car accident, and I was sure he wanted to do whatever he could to prevent the same from happening to his son.

"I'm sure your dad just wants to be as cautious as possible, so I totally get it. I would do the same for my future kids, were I to have the means." I gave him a gentle and reassuring smile so that he knew I understood.

A wave of relief spread across his face as he grabbed his suitcase and heaved it into the trunk. In went our carry-ons, and he turned around to see if I needed to put anything else back there.

"Nope, I am good to go," I said as I walked towards the passenger door. The door opened for me automatically, and I set my bag on the ground as I climbed in.

Brent slid into the driver's seat and got the heat turned on.

"Would you like your seat warmer on?"

"That would be wonderful," I replied. I was still soaking in the grandeur of this vehicle. Though I got to use a decent car regularly, this car was a level of luxury I had never really experienced before. "This car is incredible. Would definitely be a dream of mine to own one."

"Yeah, it's a really great car. It has a lot of convenient features, looks slick, and is incredibly safe. I'm really happy with it. Also, can you type your address into the GPS?"

I turned to look at the large screen that I hadn't even acknowledged yet. The map app was already open, so I typed Emma's address into the search box and pressed navigate.

"Perfect," he said. He put his car into reverse, the cameras' views popping up onto the screen. He put on some old school rock, and we jammed out singing with one another. He had a decent voice, and singing with him put me at ease. The thirty minute drive flew by, and before I knew it, we were in front of Emma's house.

Brent parked on the road near the end of the driveway since it was gated. "Let me walk you to the door."

"No, that's totally okay. I really do appreciate it though," I said as I reached across the car to give him a hug. I could feel his heart beating out of his chest as he wrapped his arms around me. At least, I hoped it was his. The hug was longer than I anticipated, but it was really nice to experience human touch outside of my mom and doctors and nurses poking and prodding me with medical equipment.

I pulled back just enough that we were face to face with about 6 inches of separation. I could feel a lump form in my throat as my nerves started to get me, so I turned around and attempted to open my door.

"It's the button on the handle," he said reassuringly.

I pressed the button and the door opened immediately, overwhelming me with the cool air outside. I had almost forgotten it was so cold out, but I quickly came back to reality as my nose went numb and my eyes hurt from the breeze. I got out of the seat and went to the trunk. It was already open and ready for me to take my bags. Somehow, Brent had gotten out of the car and made it to the trunk before I did and was pulling my stuff out for me. He smiled as he extended the handle of my suitcase while turning it towards me.

"Thank you, and thank you for the ride, too. I really appreciate it. I grabbed my stuff and walked up the pathway to the small gate and entered the code. It opened, and I started heading in. I paused, turning around to say something. "Maybe one day, I'll tell you why this meant so much," I said as a smirk crossed my face. I wasn't sure why I was teasing him, but it came out naturally. His eyes went wide as I turned around to walk up the pathway, and the gate slammed shut behind me. I could tell by the timing that he had paused before shutting the trunk and again before getting back into the car.

Before I even reached the door, my phone lit up with a text that said:

I just hope that one day, you'll trust me enough to tell me.

I turned to his car, but he had pulled away.

"Oh boy," I whispered under my breath. "What did I get myself into?"

I didn't have long to think about it as Emma yanked open the door and enveloped me in a hug.

"I missed you bestie!" She embraced me tightly, and we hugged for a few moments until she let go, grabbing me by the shoulders. "I missed you so much," she said, this time through tears.

"Oh, Emma, no crying! I missed you, too. I'm sorry we haven't spent much time together since I got out of the hospital."

"Excuse me?!" Emma exclaimed. "You are not to apologize for me being a shitty friend. I didn't visit you enough, and I should have made plans as soon as I knew you were out."

"It's totally okay, honestly. I get it—life gets in the way," I smiled at her to reassure her. "Plus, now it just means we have a lot to catch up on and can make it a night!"

She nodded in agreeance and helped me get my stuff to one of the guest rooms. It was a jack-and-jill style that shared a bathroom with Emma's room, and I was so glad to have that. It felt good to not feel completely alone or scared. Emma's family had a security guard at all times and had one of the best security systems on the market to make sure that they were safe. Her parents were both in the finance world, so this investment was a drop in the bucket for them.

After dropping my bags on my bed, we went to her room and

sat on her bed, facing one another.

"My dad added extra security details for you so we make sure you stay safe. I can't imagine how stressful everything has been for you," she said as a look of concern crossed her face and her brows furrowed. "What's been going on? Can you tell me more about any of it? I heard Nathan was arrested—is that true? I have so many questions."

"I don't think I can say much about anything since it's an ongoing investigation, but here's what I can tell you: Will is not doing well and neither is my mom, Nathan did get arrested because he's being wrongfully accused—oh, and I almost died and saw my dad when I did. So, that's great." I choked my words out, barely taking a breath. I started to sob, and Emma had me lay in her lap as she stroked my hair and rubbed my back. I hadn't considered my own feelings enough over the last few months. I needed to talk about it. I needed support from my friends. I also knew I needed to see my therapist, but scheduling an appointment with her wasn't exactly at the forefront of my mind. She was one of the best in the state and specialized in EMDR, which is something I used to get to the root of a lot of my issues with depression and anxiety.

"I'm so sorry, Olivia. Please forget I asked—I didn't mean to make you upset by asking," she offered. I could tell she was frustrated with herself for upsetting me, but it wasn't her fault. She didn't know all of the details, just the ones my mom and I chose to share.

I wanted to reassure her, but I couldn't get any words out. We sat in silence as tears continued to stream down my face relentlessly.

This was the hardest I had cried in a long time, maybe even since my dad died. As I thought about it, it made sense since I had taken on the role of being the rock for my family. I slowly drifted off, Emma still gently rubbing my head.

I jerked awake only a few minutes later, my body exhausted, but my mind wired. Emma's face showed exhaustion, her eyes barely opened, so I gently lifted myself from the bed and pulled a blanket over her. I carefully stepped around her bed on my way to the bathroom and shut the door. I grabbed my toiletry bag and brushed my teeth, put on some moisturizer, and went into my room.

I knew I wasn't going to be able to sleep for a bit, so I unpacked. As I was organizing the closet, I remembered that I had never responded to Brent's text. I crossed the bed and grabbed my phone.

"Shit," I whispered. I had forgotten to text my mom. Though that was par for the course, I quickly shot her a message so she knew I was safe.

I diverted my attention back to the message Brent had sent me:

I just hope that one day, you'll trust me enough to tell me. That sentence rang in my ears as I thought about the fact that he had been so open and honest with me, and I didn't even tell him beyond basic information about myself.

I thought about what I wanted to say back, but nothing seemed good enough. I knew I couldn't just leave him hanging, though, so I sent him something simple:

I will one day. I'll just tell you I've had enough pain to last a lifetime, and I just really don't want to add to that.

I turned on some music and went back to unpacking. I was singing along quietly when my phone started buzzing, muting my music. I walked over to my phone, wondering who could possibly be calling me at this hour.

I grabbed my phone off the bed and looked at it. I was shocked by the name flashing across my screen: Nathan. Was it really him calling? Or was it these people who had been taunting me somehow mimicking his number? Paranoia overtook me, and I didn't know whether to answer or not. Weighing me options, I knew which one I would regret more.

"Hello?" I said with hesitation.

"Olivia, it's me." His baritone voice echoed in my head. Why was he calling me? Better yet, how was he calling me? He was supposed to be in jail!

"Nathan? How are you calling me from your cell phone? I thought you were in jail?"

"I was released on bail today. My parents put the house up as collateral so I could get out. How are you doing? I saw you called my mom, so I wanted to check in and make sure you were okay." He sounded tired. I could tell it had been a long day for him, though he'd never admit it.

"Oh yeah, I'm okay. I just came back into town from Arizona. I was going to see if I could stay with your parents, but I'm staying with Emma instead since they offered and had security," I said.

"Security? Why do you need security? Is something going on?" Panic was setting in his voice.

I pressed the Facetime button on my phone so I could see his face and have a more personable conversation with him. He quickly answered, but all I could see was darkness. He turned his bedside lamp on and sat up in bed. His shirtless torso came into frame as he adjusted, and I couldn't help but notice.

"There's a lot that has happened since we last spoke. But it's been really scary for me." I hesitated to tell him details because I didn't know how he would react to the information.

"Olivia, tell me what's going on. Don't hold back—I don't care if it's terrible. I need to know." Nathan was stern, but loving. I wanted to tell him everything, but there was one of two ways it could go. He would either be upset that I hadn't informed the police, or he would tell me to wait. The former would bring the assailant to justice, and the latter would put Nathan in danger. I filled him in with what had been happening at the house and with Will being transferred to Arizona without us knowing. He learned that my mom stayed in Arizona, and that I had returned to work with my college advisors before spring came.

"Are you worried?" Nathan inquired.

I sat in thought for a moment and asked, "About what?"

"Getting into school," he replied.

"Honestly, at this point, I still have no idea what I want to do or what would be the best decision in my situation. I know my mom has reassured me about pursuing an Ivy League school, but I don't think it feels like the right decision, at least not right now. How are you doing for applications with everything going on," I paused. "I-there's something else I need to tell you, but I am scared."

Nathan looked at me through the screen, trying to read my face. "What is it?" He asked. He knew something was wrong, really wrong. "Tell me Olivia. Whatever it is—I will help you with it. But I can't help if you don't tell me."

I hesitated. Not only would I be putting my family in danger, I would be potentially putting him and his family in danger too. I didn't know if I could take that risk.

"You have to swear to me that you will not tell a soul. I need to guarantee the safety of my family and myself for as long as possible. And yours too," I pleaded with him, hoping he would agree.

"Of course. What's going on?"

I took a deep breath. "Someone is setting you up for what happened to Will, and they are threatening me with it. Threatening to hurt my mom and I if I tell anyone or go to the police. They left something on my bed, too, and I have no idea how they did it. I'm scared," I said with shakiness overtaking my voice. I looked up at the ceiling to prevent anymore tears.

"Oh, Olivia," his voice started to shake. "I am so sorry you've been going through all this. I'm so sorry I abandoned you before when you needed me most. I am sorry for all of it." Now he was crying, the pain in his voice punching me in the gut.

Instead of responding, he simply held eye contact with me. I could only imagine the amount of guilt he was putting on himself, and I knew that I wouldn't be able to pull that away from him. So instead, I just let him process everything in supportive silence.

"I know you're blaming yourself, but you absolutely cannot do that. This has nothing to do with you and everything to do with my family."

"Can I come see you?" he asked. "I know you're at Emma's, but I'd really love to see you and talk in person."

I thought about it for a moment, then nodded, telling him to message me when he got there.

"Okay, sounds good. I will be there before you know it."

We waved goodbye, and I hung up the call. I put my phone into my pocket and quietly went to the living area. I didn't think anyone would be awake at this time, so I was startled by Mrs. Grandly as I came around the corner. She looked up from her book and said, "Oh, hi honey. You're still awake? I thought you and Emma had already gone to bed."

"Emma did. I wasn't able to fall asleep, too jittery," I said shakily, smiling in hopes of deflecting from my trembling. "By the way, thank you for allowing me to stay with you guys and getting extra security. You guys absolutely did not have to do any of this, so

I really appreciate it."

"Oh, hush. You are a part of this family. You should know that by now. And the Grandly's take care of their own," she said as she reciprocated my smile. "How was your flight? Did you need something or were you just coming down to grab a snack? Can I whip up something for you?"

"The flight was fine, and I met someone that goes to a rival school. He was super nice, and apparently he is wanting to go to Yale, too." I omitted the fact that he was the one to drop me off. I didn't want to insult the amount of security they were providing me when I had been seemingly reckless. "I actually came down because Nathan is going to head over here to say hello. He was set out on bail today and wanted to talk to me about everything that has been happening. I think he feels really guilty about everything. Is that okay?"

"Oh." She paused, her face crumpling. "While I don't believe he would be capable of the charges he's facing, I'm not necessarily comfortable with you being by yourself with him. I'll have two of the security guards nearby." She was sincere but stern, taking her motherly role seriously. "While he's driving over, is there anything you'd like for a snack? I was going to make myself a grilled cheese with some soup."

Her offer was so tempting because she made the BEST grilled cheese sandwiches. As if that wasn't enough, I realized I hadn't eaten in hours, apparent by my stomach growling. "Yes, I would absolutely love one of those as well, thank you for offering."

She bookmarked her spot and got up from her seat. "You got it. One grilled cheese de Grandly coming right up!" she said, her facial expression changing into a slight smile.

I sat on one of the barstools as Mrs. Grandly grabbed all of the supplies.

"Is there any way I can help at all?" I asked.

"Not at all honey, keeping me company is enough," she responded.

While she fiddled with the stove, she cheerfully asked about my application statuses. She seemed insecure about her questioning, as though she felt hadn't been able to offer Emma much guidance. Little did she know that Emma had already applied for early admissions. I gave her advice anyway so she could feel confident in helping Emma.

As she finished up cooking, my phone buzzed. It was Nathan letting me know he had just pulled up.

"Go ahead honey. I'll put your sandwich and soup in the oven so they stay warm," she said as she gave me a warm smile.

I thanked her and walked outside. Nathan was at the end of the walkway behind the gate in his jeans and sweatshirt, looking as handsome as ever. Normally, I would have run down to him to embrace him, but something was holding me back. I opened the gate for him, and he walked onto the property. Instead of going inside, we decided to sit under some of the heaters in the backyard. We sat down on the same couch facing one another. I wondered what was on his mind in that moment, and if he could tell something was off about me. I didn't have to wonder for long, though.

"So what's going on? Why are you acting so off tonight?" He sounded genuinely concerned and confused.

"Nothing, I am just exhausted to be honest. It has been a long day," I exhaled heavily. Well, that wasn't very convincing.

"Oh, okay." He hesitated. "How is your brother doing? Any improvements with the brain bleed or responsiveness?"

"No," I responded. "He got transferred to Barrow in Arizona. So hopefully they'll figure out some things we can try to help him." I thought about Will's desperation earlier and how close he was to telling me something he witnessed. I wanted to tell Nathan, but I didn't want to get his hopes up in case Will took a turn for the worse.

"Oh really? That's awesome! When did that happen again?"

"A few days ago," I sighed, looking at the grass. I hoped he knew I didn't want to speak on it further. How was I supposed to tell him all the details about what had happened when I couldn't tell him how I knew we were being blackmailed and how I knew that he was being set up. I needed to prepare myself to come clean, but I didn't have long to contemplate that because he proceeded to ask me about it.

"So how do you know that I am being set up? Did someone say something?" A look of worry crossed his face, and it was evident that he wasn't going to just let it go.

"I am just making an assumption based off of someone hurling a rock through our window about a week ago," I lied. I did my best to keep my face even-keeled as I was one of the worst liars, and it seemed to be working.

"A rock?!" he exclaimed, shock across his face. "What do you mean a rock? Someone threw one through your window?"

"Yeah. Well, one of the glass panes in the front door. The police came to check it out but found nothing. Mom and I wanted to stop by and see Will before going to a hotel." My mind flashed back to the moment my mom and I stepped into the hospital. We were so anxious, and we hadn't even known just how absurd of a situation we were walking into. "That's when we found out that Will had been moved to Arizona—without our consent—so we headed there straight away. I think my mom just needed to have control over one thing, and seeing Will allowed her that."

He looked me in the eyes, and I could see his neck start to redden. He hung his head forward so I couldn't see his eyes anymore.

"I am so sorry," Nathan said with overwhelming angst. His remorse for everything that had happened was tangible.

"I know you feel guilty, but none of this is your fault," I said, trying to reassure him. "You can't continue to blame yourself. It's not good for either of us." I was pretty stern. I couldn't understand why I was so irritated at Nathan feeling exactly how I would in this situation, but I was.

He looked up at me, his face reddened, his eyes apologetic.

"Can we go for a walk?" he asked. He had a tendency to walk things off, so I happily obliged.

We started walking around the grounds, and I noticed that one of the security guards was close behind, as Mrs. Grandly had promised. I was grateful for that, not because I felt threatened by Nathan, but because of whoever was trying to hurt us.

We walked in silence for about ten minutes, Nathan able to slowly calm himself down in that time. We reached a ramada on the property and just stood under it, enjoying all of the lights strung up in it.

Nathan broke the silence. "I still love you Olivia. I don't think that will ever change." He looked at me as I cast my gaze down from the lights. We were a few feet apart, but he made no efforts to come close. He had always been so respectful of my boundaries.

I closed our distance and hugged him tightly around the neck. He responded by wrapping his arms tightly around my waist—as tight as he could without pain. I knew he needed this hug, but so did I. We had both been through a lot, and he was someone who could relate to my situation on a more personal level, not only because he had been by my side prior to Will's hospitalization, but also because he was facing his own issues rooted in this situation.

I pulled away, letting go of him. He let go of my waist, and I took a step back. "I'm sorry you've been involved in all of this. I'm sorry you got put in the middle. You should be focusing on college applications, not defending yourself in court."

"Olivia, just like you told me—don't apologize for this. None of it is your fault, and I would go down this path a million times again if it meant I got a minute more with you."

Ch 24

We sat in silence for a few minutes. My eyes glistened as I absorbed his words of devotion. I knew just how much he cared about me, and yet here I was, unsure of how I felt. This incredible man stood in front of me telling me he would go to hell and back for me, and I was caught up in... what?

Brent. I felt as though I had been punched in the gut. I was uncertain of my feelings towards Nathan because of some guy I just met?! What the hell was wrong with me?!

"You okay?" Nathan asked, obvious concern on his face.

"Yes, sorry. Just lost in thought. I really appreciate that. It means so much to me, but I don't want you to go through this—especially not because of me. This isn't how things should be. Besides, we never even established ourselves as a couple. How can you say all these things without having that commitment? Not only do I not want to hurt you, but I also really don't want to get hurt. You know I've been hurt enough by life, let alone love."

My response was harsh, but necessary. I had been subconsciously holding all of that in for months, and I finally got to express it to him. And while it felt good to get off my chest, I knew that it hurt him as I watched his body language change. He became very rigid and closed off, as though he knew that this topic would eventually come up but had hoped it wouldn't.

"I know. I'm sorry. I wasn't sure if you wanted a relationship in the midst of everything happening. I've wanted nothing more than a relationship with you," he responded.

"You can't tell me you're in love with me but never try to commit. That just doesn't make any sense!" I was screaming now, happy to get some of my rage out. I typically wasn't a very angry person, but when I got angry or frustrated, nothing felt better than just screaming it out.

"And then, when I needed you most, you didn't show up! You abandoned me!" I was screaming through tears now. Hot, angry tears. I was beyond infuriated. I was disappointed. I felt like when my world had been crumbling down, instead of having support in Nathan, I was alone as everything just crumbled into dust. I was angry because he disappeared, but I wasn't acknowledging that he had been dealing with his own demons before turning himself in to the police.

He wrapped his arms around my shoulders, one of them wrapping upwards around my scalp, pulling my head into his chest. He anticipated that I was on the brink of an anxiety attack even before I did, and even though I was fuming, I was so thankful for him holding me.

I promptly descended into a full anxiety attack. Shakes, sobs, palpitations, and short breaths took over me, and I struggled to focus on the calming techniques I had learned in therapy.

Fortunately, after a few minutes, my breathing returned to normal. I heard a muffled "Are you okay?" come from Nathan and just nodded my head in confirmation. Within a few moments, I felt relatively normal and calm. I gently pulled away, coming face to face with Nathan. He looked at me with such care and love in his eyes, and before I knew it, I was pulling him in for a kiss.

I felt him hesitate, taken aback by the abrupt kiss. But it didn't take him long to put his hands on my face, his fingers grasping my jawline as he pulled me in deeper. I felt a flutter in my chest as he literally took my breath away, and I was completely lost in his lips. Then, in one swift motion, he grabbed me by my hips and pushed me against one of the ramada's walls. The partially enclosed space made it easy for us to stay out of sight so the security guard was unable to see us. We were still able to enjoy the moonlight and stars, but the taller walls protected us not only from sight, but also from the cool nip of the winter winds.

Nathan pressed his body against mine as we drank each other in, and I felt myself longing for more. As if he read my mind, he slowly moved his lips from mine, kissing across my jawline, moving down to my neck. He started lifting my shirt over my head. I raised my arms, and he pulled it off with ease. He pulled his head back, looking at me.

"I love you, Olivia."

A sinking feeling engulfed me. I was back in the emotions that had led us to this point, and I didn't want to go any further when I didn't know how I felt.

"Set me down please." I asked of him, hoping to avoid a

conflict.

He set me down gently, grabbing my shirt off the ground after he did. He handed it to me, no questions asked.

"I'm going to head out. My parents are already going to be upset that I snuck out. Have a good night Olivia." And with that, he left me in my shirtless glory.

He left before my brain even had time to process it, and I didn't get a chance to explain. I quickly put my shirt back on, making sure that I turned it right side out. I ran out of the ramada, but he was nowhere in sight. However, there was my security guard standing by, far enough that he couldn't have heard anything between us, but close enough that he'd be able to take anyone down that came too close to me.

"Did you see where he went?" I asked frantically, predicting that the answer was either going to be no or that he was already gone.

Sure enough, "He's already gone, miss. He was pretty quick once he got out of the ramada. Are you ready to go back inside? I'll escort you there before heading back to my post."

I hadn't realized that I was causing him to be away from his responsibilities. "Oh, yes—I'm so sorry. I didn't realize I took you away from your assignment."

"No worries, Ms. Burke. I am here to ensure you are safe, first and foremost. Any other responsibilities are secondary to that. There's also a second security guard on duty, so we're covered," he reassured me.

I nodded to acknowledge him, and we walked back to the house. I stood in the doorway and turned around. "Thank you." I paused. I didn't even know the security guard's name.

"Seth," he smiled. "And you are most welcome, Ms. Burke. I hope you get some rest."

"I appreciate that. Thanks Seth. Have a great night, and it was wonderful meeting you," I replied, matching his smile.

I shut the door behind me and locked it, starting to head towards my room. I detoured to the kitchen, however, after remembering that Emma's mom had made me dinner. I grabbed the grilled cheese and soup and set them on the dining table. The sandwich and soup were both still perfectly warm, the cheese oozing as I took a bite. This meal was nostalgic, and I was all for it after the night I had had. I wished I could go back to my childhood before everything became so complicated. I smiled as I thought about the first time Emma and I had met, and how we'd instantly clicked and became best friends. I went to her house that same day, and her mom had made these exact sandwiches. And while we had missed out on the soup when we were younger, the sandwich was incredible on its own.

I finished my sandwich and gulped down the last spoonful of my soup, washed the dishes, then headed to bed. I laid down, and while I was full and thought I'd fall straight to sleep, my brain was wired. My mind kept replaying my night over and over again, making me more and more confused. I laid down facing up, covering my face with a pillow, wanting to do nothing but scream.

My phone buzzed, and I snatched it. It was my mom, texting me to thank me for letting her know I was safe. I guess she woke up after falling asleep and saw my message. I told her I loved her and that she should go back to sleep. She let me know that she would update me tomorrow after the doctors ran more tests on Will. Her last message read:

I love you sweetheart. Please don't ever forget that. Thank you for being so strong for both me and Will.

I set my phone on the nightstand and focused on trying to get to sleep. I quickly drifted off, fatigue finally setting in.

Ch 25

I woke up to knocking on the bathroom door. I sat up, stretching my back while telling Emma to come in.

"How'd you sleep bestie?" she asked as she stepped in the room.

"I slept pretty well actually. It's the first full night of rest that I've gotten in months, if I'm being honest. I really needed it. What time is it?"

"Oh, it's only seven. Sorry, I should have waited before waking you up," she said as she threw her head back in frustration with herself.

"No, no, it's okay. I like getting up early on weekends so I can get things done. If I sleep in too late, I always feel like I'm wasting the day. Plus, I need to run to my house. Do you think it would be okay with your parents if I brought a guard with me?"

She looked at me and rolled her eyes. "Of course, Olivia. They are here for you, no matter where you go. You should know better." She finished with a smirk, and I couldn't help but laugh. I finally felt a shred of normalcy, even with a guard protecting me.

"I'm going to go get dressed and stuff. Want me to come with you?" she asked me when she got back in the doorway.

"No, that's okay. Thank you though. I really appreciate it. I won't be too long, plus that gives you time to get ready and do whatever you need to get done." I smiled at her, and she smiled back then walked into her room.

I got up and got ready, putting on a pair of black leggings and a Hollywood Undead t-shirt. I slid my flats on, put my hair up in a ponytail, and went into the bathroom to brush my teeth. Once I was done, I headed into the kitchen where Mr. Grandly was sipping on a cup of coffee.

"Good morning, Mr. Grandly," I said very formally.

"Good morning Olivia. You know you can call my Rich, right? I know we've gone over this, but you are more than welcome to."

I looked back at him and responded before turning back to the fridge. "I know, it just feels weird. I'm not used to calling anyone by their first name, other than people my age. I just don't want to get into that habit with you and then forget and screw it up elsewhere, ya know?"

I realized how ironic it was that I was having this dialogue with him, but couldn't simply just call him Rich. I rolled my eyes at myself as I opened the fridge door, wanting to quite literally facepalm myself.

I grabbed a parfait from the fridge and closed it, turning back towards Mr. Grandly. "I am planning on stopping by the house so I can grab some of my stuff. Is it okay if I have one of the security guards come with me?"

"Oh, absolutely Olivia. But there won't be an extra one today so you'll have to wait until this evening. Is that okay?"

"Oh! No, that's okay. I should be fine going over there during the day. I'll see if Nathan will come with me. I'm sure he'd be happy to," I said through a forced smile. I knew that after last night Nathan wouldn't want to talk to me, let alone escort me into my house.

Mr. Grandly got up from the table and grabbed a set of keys from the counter. He tossed them to me. I caught them in my left hand, parfait in my right.

"Here," he said. "Go check out your new ride."

"My... what?" I asked, voice shaking. "You guys did not seriously get me a car? You've already done more than enough for me. I can't accept this." I looked down at the keys in my hand. It had the car fob and keys to the house and guest house.

"Olivia, you have been a shining light in our lives. And you have helped Emma more than she will ever admit to you. We know all about the bullying incidents and you defending her. This is the *least* we can do," he emphasized "least" as if they hadn't done a million other incredible things for me.

He gestured his head towards the door leading into the garage. "Go ahead, check it out."

I walked out of their back kitchen door and into their massive garage. I realized I had only ever seen it from the outside. It was huge, expanding a couple hundred feet at least and was riddled with nice cars. I was in disbelief as I pressed the button and the lights on a Tesla

Model X lit up. I inspected the key, realizing it was a slick version of the car, and knew I couldn't accept this. I walked back into the house, but Mr. Grandly was gone. I saw a note written on the fridge stating that all three were gone for the day and would be back for dinner.

I sighed, heading back into the garage and getting into the car. It was incredible, just as Brent's had been. The most technology I had ever had in a car was Bluetooth, and this car had all the bells and whistles. I adjusted my seats and mirrors and sat to admire the white interior. I connected my phone and turned on some music.

While connecting my phone, I acknowledged a few unread messages. There was a message from both Nathan and Brent. Nathan's read:

I'm sorry I left so abruptly last night, but I just couldn't bear knowing that you don't feel the same about me.

Brent's, on the other hand, read:

Thank you for such an amazing conversation yesterday. It means more than you know. These last couple of years have been really difficult for me, and I have definitely needed to get a lot off my chest. I hope to see you again soon.

I responded to neither. I proceeded to roll the windows down, put the car in drive and head to my house. As I pulled into my neighborhood, I turned down my music and kept my eye out for anyone I knew. I debated rolling the windows up so no one would see me, but I was enjoying the weather too much.

I pulled into the driveway and put the car in park as a police officer drove past. I was thankful that they seemed to still be canvassing the area, but I had no idea what I might be walking into. I looked in the center console to see pepper spray and a taser. They had put together a whole safety keychain for me that included not only the taser and pepper spray, but also an alarm, window breaker, and whistle. There was a note on it that read *"We love you and want you to be safe. Please keep this with you so you have at least a little bit of extra safety."*

I was so thankful for their generosity, and, as if timed, my mom texted asking to pass on her thanks as well. I told her I would, then stepped out of the car to go into the house. I unlocked the door, hearing the chime of the alarm counting down. I walked over and entered the alarm code, my accuracy confirmed by the "system disarmed" automation.

Even though the alarm had been on, something still made me feel unsettled. I couldn't put my finger on it, but something felt wrong. I ran upstairs and grabbed the essentials, stuffing it all into a duffel bag so I could get out of there as quickly as possible. As I zipped up my bag, a chill sent down my spine, sending goosebumps through my limbs. I turned around, pepper spray in hand. I didn't see anyone or anything, but I was not sticking around. I ran downstairs with my bag over my shoulder, re-set the alarm, and ran to the car, quickly slamming myself inside and locking the door.

My adrenaline was through the roof, sweat beading on my forehead as I dry heaved in my seat. I leaned forward against the wheel as I tried to calm myself. I nearly jumped out of my skin when someone knocked on the window.

I looked up to find Mrs. Holtz waving hello, a smile across her face. I rolled down my window, trying to match her composure as I attempted to lower my heart rate.

"Good morning, Olivia! How are you doing? Did you hear that Nathan is home with us?"

"Hi Mrs. Holtz. I'm doing okay, and I did. He messaged me last night that he was finally home," I said, forcing a smile in her direction.

"Oh, please do come have some breakfast with us. I'm sure Nathan would love to see you," she said, full of optimism.

Images of the night before flashed through my mind. I was certain he wouldn't, but I obviously couldn't tell her that without snitching on him sneaking out.

"Thank you for the offer, but I do have some errands I need to run unfortunately," I responded, hoping she would just let it go, but knowing better than that.

She insisted, so I reluctantly agreed. I told her I would drive over to the house and asked if she wanted to hop in.

"Actually, that would be wonderful. I went on a much further run than usual and really killed myself on it today," she said as she walked around the front of the car. I unlocked the door for her, throwing my duffel bag in the back seat as I did. She hopped in and buckled up, ready for the short trek to her house. We pulled up and parked, but just as we were about to get out of the car, she grabbed my arm and forced intense eye contact with me.

"You know how much Nathan cares about you, right?" she asked, seeming quite unsure of how I was going to answer.

"Yes, of course I do. Why do you ask?"

She let go of my arm, but continued holding my eye contact. "He has been devastated since he feels like he abandoned you while you were in the hospital. I know he was doing what your mom asked of him, but it's still eating away at him. You don't get to see him at home where he just sulks all day because he feels like he's losing you or is going to lose you. I hope that's not what's happening, but I wanted to reiterate how much he cares for you in case it is."

She got out of the car, leaving me to my thoughts. I was overwhelmed by the escalating pressure. I began packing my emotions into specific boxes, compartmentalizing for the sake of my sanity. I had gotten great at it and needed to use it to my advantage, even if it wasn't always the healthiest coping mechanism.

I took a deep breath, opened the door, and walked into the house. Mr. Holtz sat at the dining table and Nathan stood at the kitchen counter, preparing their breakfasts.

"Look who I found!" Mrs. Holtz was ecstatic to be bringing me in, not realizing the tension between myself and her son.

"Good morning, Olivia. Nice to see you," Mr. Holtz said.

"Nice to see you as well," I said with a nod and a smile.

Nathan turned towards me, looking as if he'd seen a ghost. I am sure I was the last person he expected to see this morning.

"Morning," he muttered, turning back to what he was doing. It looked like he was creating a whole platter of breakfast foods, to which my stomach responded.

"Anything I can do to help?" I asked, knowing that Nathan would refuse my assistance. Sure enough, he shook his head no and continued with prepping.

"Olivia, I'm going to go sit outside and enjoy some coffee. Care to join?" Mrs. Holtz asked. I nodded in agreement and followed her outside. Their backyard was on the smaller side, but it was beautiful, with a garden on one side and a small orchard on the other. According to Mrs. Holtz, they were trying to grow as much as they could in an effort to minimize buying fruits, vegetables and herbs from the store. Their goal was to be as sustainable as possible, and their garden was flourishing.

We sat down on the chairs outside and enjoyed the gentle weather. About ten minutes into our silence, Nathan walked out with two plates of food for us. He handed the first to his mom, then reached his arm towards me. As I grabbed it, he held on for a second longer than he needed to, looking at me with hurt eyes before turning to walk back into the house. We ate our breakfast in continued silence, and once we were done, we went inside to put the dishes in the sink. I tried to rinse mine off, but Mrs. Holtz insisted on doing the dishes herself.

"It's completely fine, Olivia. I've got the dishes. I know you had errands you needed to run, so I don't want to keep you any longer. Nathan, can you walk her out please?"

I turned to Nathan who was sitting at the table on his phone. He looked up and begrudgingly peeled himself from the chair to walk me out.

We got out to my car, and I noticed my windows were cracked and hoped it wouldn't be too cold inside. I opened the door, turning around to face Nathan. He remained silent, staring at his feet. I wasn't sure what I could say in this moment to make things better, and I had a feeling that it wouldn't have mattered. He was really hurt. But deep down, I knew he would be significantly more hurt if I were to lead him on when I wasn't sure what I really wanted.

"I'm sorry, Nathan. I hope you can forgive me for not reciprocating last night. I thought I was falling in love with you before everything happened... but now, I am not sure of anything, let alone my romantic feelings towards you. I love you, but maybe not in the way you need me to right now. The last thing I want to do is hurt you."

"It's okay, I get it. I am hard to love. Good luck, Olivia. In whatever you face. I'll be here for you as a friend, but I think I need some time and distance from you right now. I don't want to say anything I may regret because my emotions are running high." Nathan stepped forward, giving me a kiss on the forehead. "I will always love you, but I'm not going to stand by forever while you figure things out." And with that, he went inside.

I was in shock. This wasn't the Nathan that I knew and had started falling in love with. It sounded nothing like the guy who said he would stand by my side no matter what. I took a deep breath in and sat in my car, jumping from my seat because of how cold the leather was. I turned my heat and heated seats on and got away from their house as quickly as I could.

I ran some much-needed errands, including purchasing a winter jacket that actually fit, a new pair of shoes, and getting some new over-the-counter acne medication that my dermatologist recommended. The errands took me a couple hours to complete, but it was good for me to clear my mind for a bit. I decided that I wanted to treat myself to a nice late lunch/early dinner, so I headed to Monarch's Place, the local bistro that Nathan and I had gone to for our first date. Thankfully, knowing the chef had its perks.

I walked into the restaurant, and found it was busier than usual at that time of day. I scanned the crowd and facepalmed myself as I realized that it was the weekend. I had completely lost the concept of time lately, and this was just a reminder of that..

The hostess walked up about a minute later and immediately recognized me. "Hi Olivia!" she said cheerfully. "We haven't seen you around for a while. Your usual spot?"

"It's available even with how busy it is?" I asked, realizing she probably wouldn't have offered it to me if it wasn't.

"The couple that was there just cleared out a few minutes ago. I just have to get the table clean, and I can put you there."

"I would love that," I said with a smile.

She grabbed a busboy and had him go clear off the table

quickly. She came back up front and grabbed me, leading the way to the kitchen where I was able to get a full view of the staff working. I loved this table because it always amazed me how efficiently and beautifully they worked together as a team. Chef Monarch, the head chef and owner, was one of the most organized people I had ever met. He did an incredible job of managing the kitchen by investing in the top tier technology and properly educating his employees, which was a huge reason for their success—in addition to their delicious recipes, of course. I was a pretty healthy eater, and they offered nutritious dishes made with fresh and organic ingredients.

Chef Monarch walked up to me and gave me the big grin he always did when I came in. "Hi darling, how are you today? I feel like it's been ages since I've seen you."

"I'm doing okay, Chef. Thank you for asking. What's on the menu today?"

"Well, our special is wagyu, but I have a particularly special dish I'd like to put together for you. Would you be okay with that? On the house, of course," he said with a twinkle in his eye.

I nodded. "Absolutely. Hit me with your best shot," I said as I dramatically winked as if I were one of the Weasley brothers. He chuckled then went out of sight to get some ingredients for my dishes.

As the chef prepped, I pulled my phone out to finally respond to Brent:

Of course. While I am not happy about the circumstances that make us relate to each other so well, I am glad to have someone understand the difficulty of losing a parent. I know you understand the difficulty of not being able to relate to others on the subject.

After sending that message, I opened up Youtube to watch some videos, passing the time until my meal was ready. Normally, I'd enjoy the ambiance and the cooking, but today, I needed something more to distract me from my thoughts. I watched about three ten-minute videos before realizing that they weren't helping whatsoever, and set my phone back down. I diverted my focus to Chef Monarch, who was cooking and plating away. His hands were incredible, able to move at speeds with food I could only dream of accomplishing. He put the finishing garnishes on and came my way.

He had put together a beautiful array of different cuisines from all over the world, and I was excited for every part of it. Thankfully, I inherited my mom's universal love for food, and not my dad's apprehensive pickiness. My dad had always had a weird thing about textures, and it prevented him from trying a lot of different types of foods. He missed out on unique opportunities to try cuisines that were not the norm, but he didn't mind because he got to watch all of us enjoy it. It was pretty wholesome thinking back on it.

"Thank you, Chef. I'm really excited to try all of these."

He responded with a smile, then hustled back into his kitchen.

I sat peacefully eating my dishes as I watched the kitchen staff hustle to get meals out to the other guests in the restaurant. About 30 minutes later, I had finished my last dish, and I set everything back on the tray the chef had brought them on. With perfect timing, the chef emerged from behind me and set a small dessert in front of me. He gestured to the bench across from me and asked if he could sit.

"Of course! You are always welcome to—you know that!" I responded.

"I must always remain a gentleman, Olivia. You know that!" He said, mimicking me with a wink. "How have you been? I know that's rhetorical since news travels fast around here, but I want to make sure I help you in whatever way I can." His expression became somber.

I looked at him, unsure how to answer that. What could I tell him that he didn't already know and that wasn't going to get me or my family into more trouble? "I- I'm okay. I'm not great by any means, but I am also not the worst I've been over the last few weeks. Or years for that matter. I just miss my dad, he would know what to do in this situation. And if he didn't, he would just hold me and comfort me and let me know that I had an extra 'someone' there to support me through it all. And he would take some of the pressure off my mom, because I know the stress has to be killing her."

We sat in silence for a minute. Chef spoke up, "I miss your dad, too. He was such a wonderful man. I see a lot of him in you."

My eyes started to well, and I quickly wiped it away.

"Want to hear a story about your father that I have never told anyone? It was from when we were younger."

I nodded and smiled, elated that I was going to hear a secret story about my dad.

He started to tell me the story, setting the scene for the two of them in school. He talked about their classes together, how they were always causing trouble around school, and how my dad wanted to go down in infamy for his silliness. I smiled thinking back to all of the pranks that he had played on me and Will, and how he was always trying to embarrass us whenever he had the chance—like the time he came to one of my golf matches as my caddy in a hot dog costume. Thankfully, there was no dress code on that course, and I actually ended up shooting my best score and winning the tournament. My cheer quickly turned to sadness as I realized that was the last match he was able to make it to before he got sick. I missed those moments so much, and while I never felt that I had taken them for granted, I still wished I had appreciated them more in the moment.

I focused back on what Chef Monarch was saying. He was talking about one of their classes, sociology, and how they learned how to talk to people better during that class.

"Your dad had a plan to prank this girl during class. Well, little did he know, she knew of his plan. A little birdie had told her," he continued with a smirk. "And instead of him playing the prank on her, she was able to play it on him instead. One time, she put a spider in his locker and when he opened it, it fell out and he shrieked. He never lived that down, at least not in our friend group. He got her back by filling her trunk with plastic balls that poured out when she went to put her stuff away. She was a great sport and laughed it off, and it turned into a prank war until our senior year, when we went to prom. We went as a group with a lot of other people. And while we all always wondered if they would turn into anything more, we didn't think it would happen any time soon. See, your dad was a bit oblivious to people around him, let alone when someone liked him."

I listened intently to every detail he could give me about my dad—before I knew him, before he cradled me in his arms and fell in love for the second time.

"Well, that night, she must have gotten a wild hair in her because she walked up to him, grabbed him around the back of the head, and gave him a kiss. At first he was taken aback, but he grabbed her and pulled her in, finally realizing that she had the BIGGEST crush on him," he said as he gestured to show just how big her feelings were. "They went on to date for a long while. They ended up at the same college and tried to take as many similar classes as possible. They graduated together, moved in together, and eventually bought their first house together. Eventually, he got sick of that, and asked her to marry him, and, of course, she said yes. A few years later they had two of the most beautiful children one could ask for."

I matched his smile as I realized who he was talking about. My mom. That beautiful, wonderful woman was once a prankster, even though she always discouraged me and Will from doing it. Maybe she knew she would out-prank us and didn't want us feeling bad. The thought made me smile even harder.

"I had no idea my mom was so adventurous," I said as we looked at one another. "Thank you for telling me that story."

"I have way more where that came from, kiddo," he said as he got up from the bench. He came over to me and kissed me on the top of my head. He took a step back and knelt down to my height.. "Kimberly and I love you. Please don't forget that. And if you, your mom, or Will need anything at all, please let us know. We will do whatever we can to ease the burden from the loss of Andrew."

"I know, thank you. You two are always appreciated. And thank you for the lovely food. It was incredible, as always." I said, genuinely smiling. The story he told made me sad, but it also made me happy knowing that my parents had so many incredible years together.

Chef Monarch walked back into the kitchen, disappearing into one of the fridges. I took my last bite of dessert and got up from the booth. I walked towards the car, almost forgetting what I had driven there. As I grabbed the fob out of my purse, a voice emerged behind me.

"That's a nice whip you got there. How the fuck were you able to afford it?" Every bone in my body wanted to simply walk away and not acknowledge the voice, but I knew ignoring them would only serve to embolden them. I turned around, and there stood the infamous school terror, Hannah Sarver. She was known to bully, hurt people, and even get others to do her dirty business. But alas, she never got in trouble for any of it because her father was the superintendent. I hated nothing more than to have to deal with her, so I always made sure to avoid whatever paths she took at school.

"Why is it any of your business, Hannah?" I asked, being too nervous to say anything more.

"Just seems like a poor bitch like you could never afford anything like that. How many favors did you have to give to get that thing?" She asked, rude as ever.

It took me a moment to realize what she meant by favors, and I was having none of it.

"Honestly, do you not have anything better to do with your time?" I asked with a harsh tone.

"Oh honey, I have plenty I could be doing. But hurting your feelings is just a small side step to that. Don't you worry," she said with a snide wink. "Oh, how's your brother doing? Heard he's like the characters on Veggie Tales now." She cackled, truly sounding like the witch she was. My blood boiled as I walked towards her, my hands in fists by my side.

"What did you just say to me?!" I yelled, my voice cracking and my face immediately reddening. "How dare you! That's too far, even for you!"

Hannah lunged at me, fingers outstretched claws. She ripped at my hair, whipping my head down level with my midsection. I immediately stood back up and decked her in the face. Her nose collapsed on impact with my fist and blood came gushing out. That's one thing my dad taught me that I was incredibly grateful for: how to defend myself. His first piece of advice was to always let the other person throw the first punch to ensure that anything in response would be in self-defense.

Before I could get far enough away from her, she shoved me

backwards, causing me to stumble and fall. I had no way of catching myself, so I ended up going skull-first into the curb next to my car. Everything was muffled blackness. As I slowly regained consciousness, I could see Hannah's dad standing over me, ripping her a new one for what she had done. His anger and confusion revealed his obliviousness to Hannah's conduct. Apparently he had heard her comments from inside and rushed outside when Hannah turned it physical. I hoped this would lead to the end of her cruelty.

I slowly started to fade back out, faintly hearing sirens as I went unconscious.

Life moved in slow flashes. I started coming back as they rushed me down the hospital halls on a gurney. Chef Monarch's voice carried down the hallway after the doctors, confirming they could do whatever surgeries or life-saving treatments I needed. Through the chaos, I learned that Chef Monarch had been designated as my godfather, one of my father's dying wishes.

Since my mom wasn't there, Chef Monarch took over as my guardian. I was so thankful to have him in this moment, and I hoped that my mom wouldn't leave Will to come see me. Chef Monarch saw my eyes flutter and squeezed my hand, to which I tried to reciprocate. I wasn't able to, and soon, I was right back out as they pushed the propofol through my IV.

Ch 27

Hours must have passed before I woke up to the sound of beeping all around me. I had a tube coming from my mouth, again, and in my haze, I could see Chef Monarch reach from his seat to grab my hand. He gave me some comfort, reassuring me that the surgeons had controlled the bleed in my brain and made sure that my medical condition was also taken care of. I felt thankful as I started fading back out.

I could faintly hear the doctors around me, and the sounds of Chef Monarch and his wife discussing what would come next. The doctors said I would likely need to stay put and take it easy for the next couple of weeks. Other than that, it was a miracle things weren't worse.

Even though things could have been worse in that moment, I felt like I just couldn't catch a break. As if I was going to fall apart from all of these blows I kept taking. I always thought the saying "when it rains it pours" was just a cliché, but my life seemed to be a cliché-realized lately. Regardless of the torrential downpour, I knew I needed to stay positive—if not for myself, for my mom and Will.

When I finally woke up, the tube had been removed from my throat and the beeping noises had subsided. It was dark out, and instead of finding Chef Monarch and his wife, I found Emma, asleep on the lounger chair. I chose to keep quiet and let her sleep because I was sure she had a long day. A few minutes later, the Grandly's walked into the room, seeing that I was finally awake.

"Oh, Olivia! We are so glad to see you awake. How are you feeling?" Mrs. Grandly asked, waking Emma, who sprung from the lounge chair to come to the other side of my bed.

"Yes, how are you feeling?" Emma asked, her eyes welling.

"I'm okay—a little light headed—but feel pretty good all-in-all." I said, questioning what exactly I had gone through. I only knew that I had surgery to control a bleed, but I wasn't sure of any details after that. The incident was pretty hazy, and while I remembered most of it, there were definitely moments I couldn't grasp clearly.

As if reading my mind, Mr. Grandly asked, "How much do you remember? Do you feel hazy at all?"

"I think I remember most of it," I responded. "The only thing I feel right now is exhausted. I'm sure my body just needs a break from all the madness."

Mr. Grandly agreed, explaining that I was going to have to take it easy. They would be taking me home in the morning and hired on extra staff in case I needed it. I expressed my gratitude, then told them I was going to try to rest some more before my discharge the following morning. I insisted that they go home, and they obliged, after much argument from Emma. I reassured her, and she left begrudgingly, not wanting me to be alone.

After they left, I turned on the TV to watch some mindless shows to escape the real world for a bit. Though I was telling the truth that I wanted to sleep, I had felt a surge of energy since they had left. After a few episodes of Spongebob, I grabbed my phone to see if my mom had messaged me. Not only had she messaged me, but I had messages from the Monarch's, the Holtz's, including Nathan, and even Brent.

I couldn't help but open Nathan's first after we had had such a rough couple of interactions.

Sorry about your fall. Hope Hannah gets her karma.

Yet again, he didn't sound like the guy I had fallen for. It just didn't make sense that he was so off-putting towards me when he always asked me for honesty.

Instead of confronting him about it, I just responded, "Thank you, and thanks for reaching out." I didn't want to feed into the negativity. I had been doing that for so long, I just needed to continue to hold onto whatever bright side life was willing to offer before I risked losing all of my hope.

I went to my mom's messages. She had sent a bunch, first saying that she had booked her ticket home, and that she's so sorry terrible things kept happening to me. A later message said that both the Monarch's and the Grandly's insisted that she stay in Arizona with Will as she had planned while they handled it over here. She lastly said that she loved me and hoped I was feeling okay.

I reassured her that I would be fine and that I agreed she should stay in Arizona to take care of Will, and that I loved her too. I let her know I was feeling okay and that I would be going back to the

Grandly's in the morning. I knew she would be asleep, so I wasn't expecting a response, but was glad that she would have some reassurance when she woke in the morning.

I opened the Monarch's messages next.

So sorry we had to leave, Olivia. But we hope you are feeling okay and please let us know if you need absolutely anything at all. You know we will always be here for you.

I responded, saying thank you for everything, particularly for giving the doctors permission to take extensive lengths to save my life. I joked about our newfound "kinship," though I assumed the Monarch's had already known before my dad passed, or at least shortly after. I told them I'd be staying with the Grandly's, and that I'd have everything I might need.

Finally, Brent's message.

Hi beautiful soul, I hope you are having a great night. I was thinking of you today at dinner and told my dad about meeting you. He said he was glad that I met someone my age with a similar background. I hope we can hang out again soon.

My eyes welled with tears as I read this message. If I hadn't known it was from Brent, I would have thought it was that wonderful version of Nathan that I fell for, rather than his current incarnation.

I responded back, sincerely but reserved.

Hi there, it's so nice to hear from you. I'd definitely love to spend some more time with you once I am out of the hospital. I'm glad to hear that your dad approves of our newly found friendship.

I added a smiling emoji to the end to lighten up the message. I couldn't remember if I had told him about my medical history, but now he was definitely going to know.

Clearing my mind, I set my phone down on the bedside table and laid my bed back so I could try to sleep. I started to drift off after about 20 minutes, and it felt good to let my body get some much needed rest.

My dreams immediately overtook me. I started dreaming about how life used to be when I was able to just go to school and enjoy life, for the most part. When I got to hang out with my friends and play sports and focus on school rather than all of the stress and drama that was currently going on in my life. I dreamt about how happy I was and how few problems I seemed to have. About how the little things gave me the utmost joy, and I never felt I had to strain for some form of happiness. Even after my father had died, I was able to deal with my grief and still have a normal life. But these last few months were really testing my optimism that I had learned from months of therapy.

I was in a state of euphoric dreaming when I woke up with a splitting headache. I figured I just needed some pain meds since I had just undergone fairly major surgery on my head, but as I sat up, I saw blood had drained from the stent at the base of my neck onto my pillow. Worried, I buzzed the nurse's button.

A nurse rushed in, the blood rushing from her face when she

saw the blood on my pillow. "Let me grab a doctor Ms. Burke," she said as she rushed out of the room.

By the time the doctor came in, I was crying both from pain and fear by the nurse's reaction.

"Hi Ms. Burke, I am Dr. Fitzgerald. I hear you are having some drainage?"

I nodded, tears spilling from my eyes as I did.

"You are okay, this is completely normal," the doctor reassured me. "But we will get you some meds that should help. How does that sound?"

"That would be great, thank you, I really appreciate it. Does that include pain medication as well? My head seems to hurt quite a lot."

"Yes," Dr. Fitzgerald responded. "I'll make sure you got the best mix to help you as much as possible." He smiled gently as to reassure me again.

I laid back down while a pair of nurses got my medications together and silently cried into my pillow.

Based on the vials they were grabbing, the first medication they put into my line was my anticoagulant. Then followed a couple of the other medications relative to my surgery. Finally, I was given pain medication followed by anti-nausea for the most comfort. I wasn't sure what they had given me, but I immediately drifted back off as the relief went straight to my head.

I woke up the next morning to the Monarch's signing off on paperwork as the Grandly's organized all of the medications and supplies. Everyone said good morning to me and left the room so the nurses could help me into regular clothing. Once I was dressed, they helped me into a wheelchair to be taken down to the car. One of the nurses wheeled me out of the room and offered to help take me the rest of the way. The Grandly's kindly shooed her off and took over wheelchair duties.

Emma started wheeling me towards the elevator. I realized that not only did we have security personnel from the Grandly's, but we were also being followed behind by a hospital police officer. While I found that to be odd, I just figured that the Grandly's were being extra cautious.

We got to the parking structure where Mr. and Mrs. Grandly helped load me into the front seat and get me comfortable. The Monarch's walked over to the open door, and I reached over to give them a hug.

"Thank you for all that you've done for me, truly. It means so much to me and my mom. I can't thank you enough," I choked out, barely audible.

They pulled back in unison and looked at me. With red cheeks, they looked at one another, which summoned a combination of sob and chuckle. Mrs. Monarch turned back to me, taking her arm from my back and placing her hands on mine. "Of course, sweetheart. We made a promise to your dad, and we don't ever plan on breaking that. We love you and your mom dearly, and Will of course, and we would do anything for your family." She smiled through her tears as she squeezed my hands and pulled away. Mr. Monarch did the same, and they walked over to the Grandly's. They shook hands, said their thank you's and goodbyes, and walked off to their car.

I closed my door and got myself buckled as Mr. Grandly got into the driver's side and shut the door. "You still feeling okay? We will have a medical staff as soon as we get home, but I want to make sure we take care of anything you may be feeling now before we leave." I nodded and reassured him that I felt fine.

As we drove back to their house, I looked out my passenger side window at all the cars and people that were around us. I felt a ping of guilt knowing that I could never pay the Grandly's nor the Monarch's for the generosity in helping take care of me while my mom was in Arizona.

"Olivia, do you remember the first day you and Emma met? How shy you both were?" Mr. Grandly asked.

I smiled as I turned towards him. "Of course I do. We were both sitting in opposite corners, not wanting to talk to anyone." I giggled, reminiscing over why we eventually connected. "And then, go figure, we connected over helping someone with their broken wrist. Who would have thought a broken wrist would make our friendship possible?"

Eyes on the road, Mr. Grandly continued to smile before his next comment. "Well, we are very thankful that you and Emma have become such incredible friends. We love you, Olivia, as if you were our own daughter. So don't ever forget that."

"I love you all just as much," I responded, my eyes brimmed with grateful tears.

Moments later, we pulled up to the gate as it was slowly opening and drove up the driveway to the garage. There was a nurse dressed in scrubs awaiting us with a wheelchair for me. I was helped down from their car and into the wheelchair, immediately being wheeled into a room they had set up like a hospital room. It did have homey amenities, but it was definitely a very sterile environment.

"I know it's not as comfortable as a normal room, but we wanted to make sure the doctor's staff could do whatever necessary in the room without worrying about contamination. We hope this is okay," Mr. Grandly apologized, which was completely unnecessary.

"Please don't apologize, I completely appreciate that this needs to be a sterile environment. You have gone far above and beyond anything I could ever ask. I don't want you feeling bad for doing the best by me," I turned and smiled at him, and he leaned down and gave me a hug.

"Like we said on the ride home, you are just like another daughter to us, Olivia. And we couldn't imagine what we, and especially Emma, would do if anything were to happen to you. You've been a real light in our lives, and we don't take that for granted," he said, and I hugged him a little bit tighter.

We both let go, and Mrs. Grandly came to give me a kiss on the top of my head. "We truly do love you so much, Olivia. We know how hard the last few years have been for you, but we want you to know that you are loved. And we will do anything and everything to ease the pain and pressure off of you and your mom."

I grabbed her hand and squeezed it in response, afraid that I would start crying if I attempted to talk. She squeezed back, nodding in acknowledgement, and left me and Emma to hang out.

Emma and I talked nonsense while the nurse got me set up to all of the machines. She grabbed medications for my IV and put them through before leaving the room. I even had my own nurse's button set up in case I needed anything, and the whole staff was on standby in case I needed anything, including a neurologist on-call in case my symptoms changed or worsened.

Once the nurse had left, Emma turned back towards me and flashed a serious expression. "What is happening? What is going on? Why do these things keep happening? Is there more that you need to tell me?"

I looked at her, hesitating before responding. "I don't know, Emma. I don't know," I choked out. "But I know that Hannah has been bullying people for a long time, including me, so that situation doesn't really shock me."

Emma looked at my face trying to read it. "You're lying. There's something you're not telling me. Why? What's going on?" She paused, watching some of the color drain from my face. "Something serious has happened, hasn't it? Is someone blackmailing you? Is that it?"

My eyes filled with tears and fell down my face as I nodded, acknowledging her assumption.

Instead of asking more questions, she just got up from her chair, laid in the bed next to me, pulling my head into her chest, allowing me to freely sob. She had one arm behind my head, holding it, while the other was supporting my shoulder so I didn't have to strain to lay on her chest. I sobbed myself to sleep, and when I woke, it was pitch black outside. Emma had fallen asleep as well, still holding me close to her chest.

She stirred from my movement, and her eyes slowly opened. "How are you feeling?" she asked, concerned.

"I'm okay, but my head does hurt from crying so much," I said as I pressed the nurse's button.

A nurse came rushing in just a moment later asking if anything was wrong. "I just have a headache from crying, am I able to have some Advil or Tylenol?"

"Actually, you are due for a dose of all your meds and we have some pain medications within those. Does that work for you?" I agreed hesitantly. Even though I did not have an addictive personality and no addiction in my family, I still feared the possibility of becoming addicted to pain medication. I had seen too many people in my life whose lives had been ruined by drugs, so I typically avoided the risk.

The nurse walked out of the room and came back with a full carrier. She pulled out 5 different bottles and scanned them into her system to document the time and dose. She put them into my IV, starting with the pain medication that brought me immediate relief. After she emptied the last syringe, she made eye contact with me.

"Would you like something to help you sleep?" she asked sweetly. I could tell there was a genuine concern in her eyes as she asked.

"That would be great, actually," I said with a nod.

She grabbed one more vile, filled a new syringe, and put it into my IV. I immediately felt the heaviness of my limbs and eyelids hit, and Emma could feel the shift in my body as well.

"Enjoy your sleep, my wonderful best friend," she said as she got up and kissed my forehead. "I love you."

"I love..." I slurred as I passed out, unable to finish the sentence.

Ch 28

I dreamt about that night with Nathan on the Grandly's property—about how happy I was to be with Nathan, and the sheer panic I felt when I knew I had to be honest with him. And the pain that fell across his face when I was. I hated it. I was seeing the situation from a third person's view, and it was beyond painful. It was unbearable. Maybe I couldn't blame Nathan for how he was treating me. But I really felt hurt by his actions as he had always asked me to be honest with him, no matter how badly it would hurt. I was so used to people saying those types of things and never following through. But as cliché as it felt, I really did think he was different. And I needed to get over the fact that he wasn't.

Towards the end of the dream, as I watched Nathan walk away, I got an odd feeling. It almost felt as if I wasn't alone in watching him. I felt a chill run down my spine as an invisible shadow cast over me. I jerked awake to find Emma standing next to the bed looking at me. "Holy shit!" I screamed, frightened but relieved it was only Emma.

"Sorry!" she exclaimed as she jumped back. "Definitely did not mean to scare you. I was just debating if I should let you sleep or see if you wanted some brunch."

"Brunch? Aren't you supposed to be at school?" I asked, knowing that finals were coming up.

"Don't you worry about me. I've got it all under control," she said emphasizing the "all" and adding a smile. "All of my teachers are aware of my current situation, and yours for that matter, and we'll be just fine."

I thought about that for a moment and looked up at her. "Well, brunch it is, then."

I slowly got up from the bed, realizing that my equilibrium was not where it needed to be. Emma grabbed my arm in hers, grabbed my IV bag stand in her free hand, and helped me get to the bathroom. I was able to lean on the counter to keep me balanced as I got ready for the day, washing my face and brushing my teeth. In the meantime, Emma was grabbing me some comfortable clothes to wear. She walked back into the bathroom and set them on the counter, looking at me as she did. "Do you want or need to take a shower? I can grab the nurse?"

I shook my head and said, "No, not right now. Thank you though. I'll take one after brunch."

She helped me get dressed, both of us struggling to put the fluids bag through my sleeve. Once I was ready to go, we went over to the kitchen, where a beautifully prepared meal was sitting on the table. It was covered in all sorts of dishes from waffles to fruit to bacon to eggs, and I couldn't be more excited to eat. I noticed just how hungry I was as I looked at all of the food in front of me, and I quickly sat down.

I indulged my hunger, eating far too much. Once Emma and I

were both finished, one of the nurses helped me outside, and we got comfortable in one of the ramadas on an outdoor couch.

We talked about the weeks leading up to my hospital stay. We shared laughter and tears as if we hadn't seen each other in years. It was so nice to reconnect with my best friend this way.

My head started hurting, but I ignored it since I figured I would just need another dose of medications. But as the minutes passed by, I could feel my face start to flush, and Emma noticed the color start to fade from my face.

"Olivia, are you okay?" she asked as she got up from the other side of the couch. She caught me as I started to slump over. I immediately started vomiting all over the ground as Emma screamed for the nurse.

The nurse grabbed a wheelchair and bucket, but before she could reach me, I let out the most blood curdling scream as the pain in my head became unbearable. They both helped lift me into the chair as the nurse placed the bucket on my lap. I had my hands on my head and squeezed my temples, trying to give myself any possible relief. As they wheeled me back toward the house, I continued to vomit all of the food I had had that morning. Most of it was still undigested, and I couldn't successfully regurgitate enough to breathe. I could feel the food catch as it forced its way towards my mouth, only allowing me to make choking gasps. I started to sob, which didn't help my situation whatsoever.

The nurse got me back into the room, and between her and the doctor, they were able to get me onto my bed. The nurse darted from the room and returned as quickly with equipment and medication. She got each syringe prepared as the doctor checked them and injected their contents into my IV. I wasn't sure what was happening beyond that. My main focus was emptying my stomach so I could breathe again.

As the doctor pushed the medications into my IV, I felt the pressure in my head relieve along with my nausea. But the last medication he put through was different from any of the others. It was milky, resembling propofol. I wondered why he would be giving me that, but I didn't have any time to question it as I started to lose consciousness. I could hear the doctor talking to me, asking me questions.

"Olivia, does your head still hurt?" I was barely able to nod in response. "Okay, we're going to look in your stent to make sure there's no blockage. It might be uncomfortable, but just know that this is in your best interest."

He grabbed something from the rolling tray. "This is a camera so I can see inside the stent, and it has clamps so that I can grab anything in the way. And just so you know, I gave propofol because, even though the brain doesn't have nerves to feel pain, we need you to be as still as possible so we don't cause any additional damage." He paused, adjusting the neck of the camera. "Okay, we are going in, Olivia."

I could feel the movement around the stent as panic grew in my chest, but I was unable to calm myself. And though I was panicking on the inside, my mind and body started to drift. "Stay with me Olivia," the doctor said. My thoughts immediately went to Emma, and I was concerned for her mental well-being watching this scene unfold. "We need to make sure that we don't cause any pain or discomfort. The device is in. We found a clot that is blocking the drainage from the stent. I am going to grab it now so we are almost good to go."

Silence overtook the room, and I could feel the device slip out of the stent. "I got the blockage, Olivia. The pressure in your head should start relieving here shortly," the doctor said as he held the clot in my line of sight. It seemed to be a fairly large clot, significantly larger than the tip of the instrument used to pull it out. The doctor, still holding onto the syringe that had the propofol, started squeezing the rest into my IV.

"We need to shut your brain off for a little bit," he explained. "This will help your body reset."

Before he was able to inject the vial's full contents, I reached out to Emma. She ran over and grabbed my hand and squeezed. I responded by mustering the minimal squeeze I was able to. "I love you Olivia, you're going to be okay. I promise. Please don't give up," she said, and that was all that I heard as I fell into darkness.

Ch 29

I woke up in the park. I braced myself, fully expecting to see the fire engulfing the playground. But instead, it was the peaceful park I had grown up in.

I walked around, taking in my surroundings as I did. Everything was just as it had been 10 years ago—not a swing or bar burned. The slides were my favorite shade of blue, and the structure was primarily lime green with turquoise and orange accents.

The wave of nostalgia was beyond overpowering, and I felt a significant sense of peace. I remembered all of the winters that were spent in that park, the white creating a gorgeous "winter wonderland" for all of us kids. There were ramadas with benches that would protect us from getting soaked when it would start pouring—we would never heed our parents' warnings. The trees slowly transitioned to bright yellow, the color of our falls. It was all so serene, and the warmth continued to spread throughout my body as those memories softly bounced around my brain.

My dream told me that I had been sitting in a swing during these observations. I looked up to see a boy in the distance next to some of the trees. I couldn't see what he was doing, so I got up to move closer. He had a rock in his left hand and steadied himself against the tree with his right. It appeared he was carving into the tree, but I couldn't see his design. The wind wisped through the naturally highlighted locks of the figure that stood before me. I recognized both the hair and the stance the figure took: Nathan.

There was no way, right? There was no chance I was watching the moment that Nathan was carving our letters into the tree all those years ago. Even though the child wasn't able to see me, I still felt like I would disturb his flow if I came too close, so I walked to the other side of the tree while maintaining my distance. Sure enough, there was the "N" carved into the tree, but he hadn't yet carved my initial, or anything else for that matter.

I walked closer to the tree to find that Nathan was singing to himself. I was able to pick up on the lyrics he was singing, and they were to "You and Me" by Lifehouse. As I stood there listening, he sang, "What are the things that I want to say, just aren't coming out right? I'm tripping on words, you got my head spinning, I don't know where to go from here." He continued on to the chorus, and my chest swelled, my windpipe tightened, and my eyes burned.

I joined in his singing softly, so as not to disturb him: "And of all the people, and I don't know why, I can't keep my eyes off of you." I continued to sing, not realizing he had stopped. I opened my eyes, snapping out of the groove I was in. Nathan had turned around and was staring right at me.

I could feel myself panic as I tried to figure out how he was seeing me. He dropped the rock he had been carving with and started towards me. My mind started to panic as I realized how close he was, and I didn't know if I should open my arms for an embrace or just brace myself. I did neither as he ran past me to a group of kids getting out of an SUV. It must have been a birthday party because the parents had a bunch of balloons and presents.

Nathan ran up to the SUV and stopped short by about a few feet. "Hi Mrs. Langston, what can I grab for you?"

"Oh, Nathan, sweetheart, can you grab the cake out from the front seat? That would be such a help for me."

He happily grabbed the cake and took it to one of the ramadas where they started setting up for the party. Some time went by, then kids started filtering into the party, one of them being Will. I quickly figured out that this was a birthday party for one of Will's best friends, which made me wonder why Nathan was there. I quickly learned that the birthday boy had an older brother that was close friends with Nathan. I realized just how small our circle was in that moment, and while it made me appreciate the close-knit family I had gotten within the community, it also made me feel like a pretty horrible person. Nathan was right here, and I hadn't known it. It made me cringe to imagine that we had been at the same parties and that I had never noticed him, or that I just didn't remember him.

My fear became reality when I watched my mom's car pull up into a parking place. She got out of the car, as did I, and we headed towards the ramadas to pick up Will. As we approached, I turned to watch the reaction of anyone else. Sure enough, there was Nathan, his eyes lighting up when he saw me. He ran up to my mom, putting his hand out to shake hers.

"Hi Mrs. Burke, I hope you're doing well today. Will is over by the weird swing thing," he said as he shook her hand.

"Thank you, Nathan. I appreciate that update," she said, shaking his hand back. She then turned to me and asked, "Are you okay if I go grab him and talk to the Langston's real quick?" I nodded, and she scurried off to collect Will and talk to all of the other parents.

"Hi, I'm Nathan," he said, reaching his hand out to 12-year-old me. I watched myself shyly grab his hand and give it a little shake.

"I'm Olivia, nice to meet you," I said, awkwardly avoiding eye contact.

"You too," he said. The conversation didn't go anywhere from there as I saw my young self sink into my turtle shell. I had come along a long way from this shy, introverted little girl. She wouldn't recognize the nearly 18-year-old young woman who couldn't care less what others thought of her because, at the end of the day, you only have yourself. I always made sure to remind myself that I should only want people around me that love me for me and that nobody should expect me to act differently or change just because I may be a little "weird" some days.

The feeling of dread I had earlier vanished as I remembered that version of myself. I had blocked out as many memories of her so that I could avoid reliving my dad's decline.

Thankfully, this awkward scene ended quickly as my mom came back over, grabbed me, said goodbye to Nathan, and led me and Will to the car.

Nathan waved goodbye as we walked away from him, and a

small but noticeable smile spread across his face.

"Nathan! Why are you smiling for?" his friend asked as he ran up to Nathan.

Nathan's face became bright red as he looked at his friend to answer. "Oh, Mrs. Burke just said my shoes are cool," he responded as he looked down at his feet.

Apparently this answer satisfied his friend because he grabbed Nathan's wrist to pull him towards the presents. I thought for a moment and realized that my mom must have purposefully grabbed Will when she did to avoid the gift part of the day.

My mom had always made it a point to not open presents in front of everyone, and subsequently, not to be a guest at a party where it was occurring. Her reasoning was simple: people shouldn't have to pretend they like things when they don't in order to spare their friends' feelings. It's not fair to ask a young child to be able to control their emotions well enough to not hurt someone's feelings.

This was one of the weirder family traditions we had, but I loved having that mindset. It avoided hurt feelings while also avoiding jealousy. It also prevented children from feeling bad if their parents couldn't afford the things their friends were getting. I missed out on significant chunks of parties when I was younger, and I would always get so angry with my mom for not allowing me to stay. But now, I was able to appreciate it both firsthand and secondhand.

I watched the rest of the party happen and then all of the kids packed up and left with their parents. As I surveyed the scene, I found

Nathan back at the tree he had been carving. He had the rock up to the tree again, and it looked as if he was finishing his carving. He had added a plus sign below his initial, but instead of putting mine, he set the rock down and sat down under the tree. I could hear him mumbling to himself, but I couldn't quite understand what he was saying. Before I was able to get closer to him, everything faded away.

Ch 30

I opened my eyes, this time in a hospital hallway. As I tried to figure out exactly where I was, I heard my own voice emerge from around the corner. I was dressed in my hospital gown, towing my IV stand behind me, and entering Will's room. I followed closely behind because there had to be some reason I was back in this moment, right? Was it the day I cried at his bedside? Or possibly the day of the code blue? Either way, I couldn't imagine my subconscious taking me here without there being a reason for it.

I surveyed the room, trying to remember exactly when this was. But then I saw it, the elephant that I had given to Will before he grabbed my hand. Time passed, and I watched myself cry as I laid my head next to Will. Memories of dread started to overtake me again as I felt a piece of my soul break off.... I knew that even a small part of him was still there, but I didn't know if it was enough to help bring him back.

Then it happened—I watched from a secondhand perspective as Will squeezed my hand. The joy of that moment was palpable even in my dream state. I watched as the nurses and doctors filtered in, reliving everything they had said to me in that moment. But one thing was different. I could hear the staff talking as they congregated outside of the door.

"That kid is as brain dead as it gets. Not a chance he is coming back from this," the doctor said bluntly to one of the nurses.

"Did you still want me to document the activity, doctor?" the nurse said with a smirk. No one else seemed to notice except the doctor in question, which escalated my anxiety. This was the same nurse who revelled in my pain when I was in the hospital, and now, instead of doing her job, she was seemingly flirting with the doctor who had lied to my mother.

"No, don't bother. It's not of any significance. It was likely just a spontaneous body movement that happens within comas. Let's go see the next patient," the doctor said, lacking all of the compassion he should have for pediatric patients.

I wondered if they would say anything more about Will, so I followed them into the next room. However, there was no patient, just an empty bed and chairs. I found this to be odd, and as I put two and two together, the doctor started kissing the nurse.

And in the next moment, I was awake. I reached blindly towards the nightstand, grabbing for my journal to write what I had just witnessed. Emma was sitting on the couch in the room and shot up from it as she saw me grasping around.

"You're okay, you're okay! You just woke up."

"My journal, I need my journal, Emma. Please. It's important," I said frantically.

She nodded, and quickly found it next to the bed. She grabbed the journal and found me a pen and handed them to me. I started writing feverishly so I could get all of the details down that I possibly could. I started out with the hospital incidents because I felt those were the most important, especially if they were valid. This information could potentially give my mom an even better case if she wanted to pursue malpractice against the hospital.

I wrote down everything that was said, but I also took note of the nurses and doctors that were all within the vicinity of what was being said. I wrote down descriptions of their scrubs, their hairstyles, anything that would be identifiable. I needed as much information as I could because I just knew it would be important.

Once I finished writing about the hospital, I took a few notes about that day at the park with Nathan because I had so many questions for not only him, but myself. How could I forget that day? I know it seemed unimportant, but I never, *ever* forgot a face.

Before Emma could say a word, I looked up from my journal, slammed it shut, and set it on the bed next to me. "Have you ever just completely forgotten someone that you met?" I asked, furrowing my brow.

"I'm not sure I understand what you mean. Like, someone who you met briefly, actually was introduced to, what?" she asked, curiously striking her face.

"Like someone that you spoke to, might have been part of your life. That you see all the time around your family and friends?" I could feel the look of concern spread across my face, coupling with my already furrowed brows.

"Probably not, why? What did you see?" she asked, truly

wondering.

Emma knew that I had a history of seeing or dreaming things that were too coincidental. Most of the time, it was small things. But growing up, there were a couple times that I "saw" something in my dreams that didn't make any sense up front, and that didn't seem plausible, so we just brushed them off. One of the times, I had seen a vision that showed a neighbor cheating on her husband. While I had never even met them, I saw the wife at someone else's home. Sure enough, a couple weeks later, the husband had moved everything out to the lawn, and she and her new man came to pick up everything. It had been the exact same man I saw her with in my dream. I brushed it off then as a coincidence, that maybe I had just seen him come to her house some time and put two and two together.

It happened again sophomore year. I convinced a classmate to spend time with me instead of going to a football game on a hunch. Sure enough, an accident from my nightmare happened at one of the nearby, major intersections. Three people had been killed, and seven additional people had been injured. It happened at the exact moment they would have been at that intersection had they left on time, and it shook me to my core. I knew then, as did Emma, that this was not something I could take lightly.

Though I had believed in my dreams before, I was hesitant now. Seeing both Nathan and the hospital staff made me doubt the truth of my dreams. There was no way this could be true; these were past events, one of which was nearly ten years prior. But what if they were? What if I was really seeing these situations, as they happened, to be able to process them from a different perspective?

Emma fully connected the dots and came to sit on the bed next to me. She looked me in the eyes, grabbed my hands, and sat in silence with me.

"I saw Nathan, as a child. And it was the day that I apparently met him," I said as I lifted my head to make eye contact with her. "But…" I trailed off, becoming lost in my thoughts again.

"But what? Olivia, what did you see?" I could see some of the color drain from her face as she realized how serious I was.

"I saw... I saw myself. In third person. Which wouldn't be as weird if I hadn't seen Nathan when I wasn't part of the scene at all. It would be one thing if I was remembering things or seeing things from third person that I had actually witnessed in real life. But seeing Nathan do things that I never actually witnessed myself is really unnerving," I responded, trying to read her face.

"Like what kind of things?" she responded, not missing a beat.

"Like when he carved his initial into the tree."

"His? As in, he didn't carve yours?" she asked.

"Nope. He carved his own initial and the plus sign, but that was it. He was saying something to himself, or possibly the tree, after he did that, but he left without carving my initial," I was realizing just how weird this story was sounding, but I knew there had to be some truth to it. I just wasn't sure what that was yet. "I know this all sounds so bizarre, and I recognize that. But something just seems... " I trailed off again, looking for the right words.

"So real? Like there's no way that this could be fake?" she asked, immediately sending me into a flashback of when she said those exact words to me in third grade. I remember her standing by my side when I thought I wasn't going to keep any of my friends because I felt so different. Instead, I was able to rely on her to get me through the harder days when I felt crazy for thinking my dreams to be true. I was scared of experiencing these dreams on such an intricate level again, but I found a significant amount of comfort in knowing that Emma was continuing to stand by my side and wasn't scared of or frustrated with me.

Waves of emotions poured through me as I realized that there was a huge possibility in these dreams being true. I couldn't react. I had gone numb. I took some deep breaths as Emma adjusted herself to be able to rub my back.

"It's going to be okay. I will be here, just as I have been forever, promise," she said as she held out her pinky. The age old "pinky promise" that never became obsolete between us and that we had never broken. We rarely used it, but we had used it enough that we really valued the promise that backed it. I gripped her pinky with mine, then pulled her in for a hug as I started to sob. It was as if every emotion had hit all at once, and I couldn't stop how it manifested. I could feel my body trembling as I sobbed, Emma holding on to me as tightly as she possibly could, knowing that I was on the verge of a panic attack. I hadn't had one in so long that I had almost forgotten the signs. But Emma, being the incredible friend she was, knew from a mile away that it was coming.

Emma was successful in calming me enough to avoid a panic attack, but I continued to shake profusely. Emma grabbed the journal to read, and I let her because there was no need to keep it a secret, at least not from her. She started reading, and from the first word, I could tell she was entranced by what I had written. Her jaw quite literally started dropping as she continued reading in disbelief, just as I had felt in my "dreams."

We talked for a little while longer and asked a few questions. While we were both in disbelief, yet again, everything made sense. There were no parts of the stories that didn't line up. The longer I dwelled, the weaker my grip on reality seemed to become. I just needed to keep my journal close by so I could have my mom read my entry whenever I saw her next. And while I could have sent her a picture, the entries were private, and I couldn't risk the possibility of them getting into the wrong hands.

Once the conversation tapered off, I told Emma to go have fun and relax and not worry about me. I knew she needed a break from taking care of me, and she deserved to go spend time with our other friends. She asked if I was sure, to which I reassured her, and she left to go work on some homework before heading out.

After she left, I grabbed my phone, noticing it had blown up since I had gone to sleep. Most of the messages were from my mom, which was understandable, and it was a roller coaster. It started out with her worrying about why I wasn't responding, panicking and yet again saying that she was going to come back to Oregon, to her saying that she wasn't coming per the reassurance of the doctors that were taking care of me. I messaged her back, apologizing for causing extra stress and telling her just how much I loved and appreciated her. I felt she hadn't heard that enough since my dad passed away, and now I was the only one who was able to say those words to her. She needed reassurance more than anything right now, and that was the least I could do with her being hundreds of miles away. I knew I wouldn't be able to take away her guilt, but I wanted to alleviate as much of the negative emotion as possible. Will needed someone to fight for him right now, while I just needed good doctors because I had my community in my corner.

I had a message from the Monarch's that read:

We hope you are doing okay, please let us know if there is absolutely anything we can do for you.

I smiled, appreciative of how sweet they were to me. I thanked them and assured them that I would certainly do that if anything came up.

Once I sent that message, I noticed I still had a few more left, and even though I didn't feel up to talking to anyone, I decided to respond instead of making anyone wait any longer. One of the messages was from Emma, before I had woken up, telling me just how much she loved me, how she couldn't do life without me, and that I had to be okay. Even though I already knew everything she had put in that message, it still felt comforting to see it all written down. I would cherish that message forever.

There were two messages left, and both of them were from Brent. He had asked me why I was in the hospital, and then he sent a follow up message saying that I didn't have to explain anything to him that I wasn't comfortable and that he would listen whenever I felt ready.

Instead of messaging him back, I decided to call him and hear his voice. I felt his patience warranted at least some explanation.

"Olivia? You're okay?" The relief was audible, even shaky.

"Okay is a relative term, but yeah, I could definitely be worse," I responded. Then,

before I could stop myself: "Would you want to come over here and talk in person? I'd have to stay pretty stagnant, but I'd really like to tell you everything in person."

A pause on the other end of the phone caused my anxiety to rise. "Of course, I do have a couple of things I really need to finish that I've been procrastinating, but I will be there as soon as I am done. Same house I dropped you off at?"

"Yes, I'll let the gate know you're here for me," I said, knowing security was at an all time high. We hung up, and I went back to my thoughts.

One thing I hadn't thought about in a while was my house. Was it even still standing with these people out there threatening us? I asked the nurse if they could grab either one of the Grandly's, and Mrs. Grandly came rushing in.

"Everything okay, Olivia?" her face flushed from rushing to my room.

"Oh my gosh, I'm so sorry. I didn't mean to give you a scare," I said, seriously concerned for the stress I had just caused her. "I just wanted to ask if you knew anything about our house and what's going on with it?"

"Oh, honey," she exhaled in relief. "No worry at all. We have had a security detail on it any time the cops are not keeping an eye on it. It's safe, and no one has even dared to approach it since you've been with us." She smiled, and though the information itself was comforting, I had an unsettled feeling that I could not shake.

"Are you serious?" I asked, my voice trembling as I felt myself on the verge of tears. "You guys seriously do not have to do that, you are doing far too much. And I appreciate it more than you will ever know."

Mrs. Grandly embraced me in a hug, and I reciprocated as I leaned into her shoulder. But I was quickly pulled out of my teariness and let out a giggle as I said, "So this is what it means to have a shoulder to cry on huh?"

We both started to laugh and she pulled away, wiping away her own tears as she did. "I guess you're right," she said, the relief apparent on her face. "Is there anything else you need right now? I have to go do a few things for work but want to make sure you're taken care of since I know Emma is going to be leaving in a bit."

"No, seriously, you both have done more than enough. I do

want to ask though, is it okay if I have a friend come over? I have some explaining I need to do with him," I asked, wanting to be respectful of their home even though I already knew the answer.

"Of course, Olivia. You know that you are more than welcome to most things in this household. But dare I ask why you have explaining to do?" she asked, raising her eyebrow.

"I told him about me being at the hospital without any context. He doesn't know any of my story, so he's really in the dark. But, thankfully, he's being incredibly respectful of it." A thought came to mind. "Oh, did the doctor say I was able to go for a walk or not? I'd really like to do that if possible," I said, unsure of what the answer was going to be since my last little walk didn't end well.

"He said you could resume light activity once you woke up, so I don't see that as a problem. Just make sure the nursing staff is aware of what you are doing so they can help you if you need," she responded, getting ready to leave.

"Thank you Mrs. Grandly, for everything. I appreciate each and every one of you," I said as I smiled, trying to hide any tears that were trying to make their way from my eyes.

"You are absolutely welcome, sweetheart. I'll always remind you of this, but I just never want you to forget that you are like a second daughter to us."

"I won't," I said, and with that, she left.

Ch 31

I decided I would try to shower before Brent got there, and while I wanted to do it by myself, I knew it would be smarter and safer to have a nurse help me. She got me into the shower, and lo and behold there was a chair in there for me to sit on. I was thankful because I wanted to be able to save as much energy as possible for a walk with Brent. I got myself cleaned off, being careful around my neck and the stent that was there. I wasn't able to wash my hair, but just washing my body was enough for me.

I stepped out of the shower feeling refreshed and got dressed into a new set of pajamas that smelled like fresh linen and were warmed for me. I wasn't used to all of these privileges I was experiencing, and while they weren't necessary, I revelled in them. I did my hair in a bun as best as I could and brushed my teeth, desperate to feel myself again.

I could feel my phone start to vibrate in my pocket and went to pull it out as Emma walked into the room. I left the phone in my pocket and turned to her. "Everything okay?" I asked, confused while she was still there.

"Are you sure you're okay with me leaving? I can stay in with you. Or we can go do something together?" she asked, clearly concerned about leaving me alone with my thoughts.

"Yes! I'm totally sure. Please go enjoy yourself. You've been an incredible friend to me, the least you can do for yourself is have a night off from stressing out about me," I said, genuinely smiling. I meant what I said because she had been beyond just a good friend. She was a sister, a best friend, and a part of my soul, and I couldn't live with myself if I ever held her back. "Plus, Brent is going to come over here so I can tell him about my wonderful hospital stay. I left him a message that gave him zero percent context and one hundred percent anxiety," I commented, laughing.

She giggled in response, "Well, I'm glad you're getting your mind off of things. I love you, Livs," she said as she hugged me. I squeezed back, acknowledging her love for me while also telling her I loved her too.

As she gently closed the door behind her, my phone started buzzing again. It was my Mom. I answered, cringing as I did, expecting the worst.

"Mom, hi! How are you? Is everything okay?"

"Oh, yes honey, sorry, I didn't mean to scare you or anything. I just had some down time and wanted to call you, see how you're doing," she responded, relief sweeping across me.

"Would you want to Facetime so we can actually see one another? I really miss seeing your face."

"Oh, Olivia, that would be wonderful. I miss seeing yours, too. Can we do that from our phone call, or do we have to hang up and reconnect?" she asked, relying on my knowledge of technology.

"We don't need to hang up, I'll push the button to convert this to a Facetime and you just have to accept it like you would a normal phone call," I explained, hoping that would be enough information for her to figure out how to do it.

I pressed the button and held the phone so that she could see my face. My mom's face popped up on the screen as she accepted, and we both showed huge grins that dissolved into desperate tears.

"Oh, baby, I miss you so much. I'm so sorry I haven't been able to be there for you lately. I feel horribly for that. I know you told me that I shouldn't, but I just can't help myself. I want you to know just how much I love you and that in any other circumstance, I would be right by your side. This time has been way harder than when your father passed. At least I was prepared for handling that, this has been a complete shit show of me feeling like a failure of a parent," she paused. I wanted to give her a moment in case she kept going so that she could really vent to me. "Dammit, I'm sorry Olivia. Here I am making it about myself when I should be focused on you and how you're doing. How are you doing, baby? Do you need anything from me that I can provide? Do you need me to come see you?"

"Mom, mom, mom," I repeated over and over until she stopped talking. "I'm serious, you need to stop worrying about me and focus your energy on Will. I know that is easier said than done, but you need to focus on him. I have everything I need here. Even more. You are beyond stressed right now, it's not healthy for you. You'll end up in the hospital next if you keep going at this pace."

She looked down from the camera, then back at it. "I know, I know, I really need to take a few steps back and slow down, but some days that just feels impossible."

I could tell she was trying not to break down, so I changed topics. "Mom, I've been meaning to talk to you about this. But Nathan has been acting weird."

"Weird how?" she asked, my distraction tactic working.

"He just doesn't seem himself. He's been really harsh and just not wanting anything to do with me. I am having a hard time understanding what happened to the loving guy who said he'd stay by my side no matter what happened. It's just such a drastic change. And I just truly don't get it," I said, pausing. And even though I knew it wasn't my doing, I couldn't stop the next words from coming out of my mouth. "Did I do something wrong?"

"When did this start? Because if it's recent, do you think it's because of the things I said to him when you were in the hospital? Maybe he still feels I don't want him around you?" Her questions made it evident that she felt incredibly guilty for making him stay away from me under false pretenses.

"Mom, no, I definitely don't think it has to do with that. I sort of turned him down in a way," I replied.

"What do you mean sort of?" she asked, her tone shifted to curiosity.

"I told him that I cared about him but that I needed to focus on myself and my health and family, and that I wasn't sure where I stood with him. We always said we would be honest with one another and not lead each other on if either of us felt something was off or we didn't feel the same. But he basically did a complete 180 of that, and I just don't understand what made him change so drastically," I explained, hoping she wouldn't ask for any other details.

"Maybe he just feels a bit abandoned? But he's definitely taking that out on you unfairly if that's the case. Other than that, I honestly have no idea. He's a good kid, at least from what I've seen. So I do find it odd that he's being like that, especially if he said all those things to you and promised you better. Do you want me to talk to his mom? I can ask her if she knows what's going on?" My mom genuinely cared and wanted to get me answers, but that wasn't how I wanted to get them. I knew that this was something I would need to handle on my own, but I appreciated being able to talk to her about it.

We continued to talk for over an hour, and it was nice to catch up with her. There was no progress on Will, but there was also no regression. He was steady, and right now, that was a positive sign to the doctors. They had feared he would start regressing and that he wouldn't be able to recover if he did. She continued by telling me about the doctors and nurses and how all of the staff was absolutely wonderful. My dream flashed into my head as she was telling me this, but I knew that she would have a hard time believing me. I had never told her that my "visions" were a recurring event.

I realized she had paused and was looking at me intently. "What's going through your head? I see you're deep in thought, so don't bother denying or saying 'nothing,'" she said, concern washing over her face again.

I cleared my airway, feeling it tighten as stress overcame me.

"I—mom. Do you remember when I told you about the dream I had when I was younger? That it felt so real and ended up coming true?"

"Yes?" she questioned, not understanding where I was going with this.

"I had another one, but this time, it was about the staff at the hospital," I responded. "It's also not the first time it's happened since I last told you about it. There have been a lot of things that have happened over the years that I mostly brushed off as coincidence, and you had enough on your plate as it was. The last thing you needed was having a daughter who was seeing shit," I said, looking down at the ground, embarrassed that I was just now telling her all of this.

"Oh, Olivia, I wish you didn't feel that way. I want you to come to me with anything, no matter how bizarre sounding it is. Trust me, I have had moments like that too where I question if something that occurred was a happenstance or if it really was me seeing something that was like a vision. How many times have you experienced this? And what happened this time?" Her concern turned to relief and questioning.

"I honestly couldn't tell you an exact number, but it's probably at least twenty? And, obviously, this time it had to do with the hospital staff here in Oregon that took care of Will. I think there are some sketchy things happening in that hospital, at least in that particular pediatric sector," I said, cringing at the idea.

"Tell me more. I want to know everything. And I absolutely believe you saw these things for a reason," she said with conviction.

"I need to know every detail you can possibly remember."

"Of course, let me grab my journal. I wrote it all down," I said.

"That's my girl, always resourceful," my mom replied, a smile spreading across her face. "Your father taught you well to document everything. I guess his cancer really did have some positives." She was still smiling, though I could see the pain behind her eyes as she did. I knew it hurt her to talk about my father, but I was so glad she was making progress in doing so. A couple of years ago, she'd been reluctant to acknowledge him in fear of hurting us. Now, she was able to unsurface silver linings in his suffering.

I grabbed the journal from the nightstand and started reading. I explained things as I remembered them and added notes while she jotted down her own. My mother's face never gave away a hint of shock as my vision unfolded. I finished, then asked her why she didn't seem surprised.

"I know some ladies who work in the hospital, specifically in the NICU, and they have said some of the nurses and doctors are inept and/or don't do their jobs properly and take the easy way out when they do. The one thing that I hadn't heard about was inappropriate relationships. Those ladies said it is strictly forbidden to fraternize or date another employee in the hospital in order to keep the focus on patients. They even sign documentation stating they won't," my mom explained, sparking my curiosity.

"Uhhhh," I responded, pausing. "May I ask why they shared that information to you?" I asked while stifling a bit of a laugh. My mom was always good at getting people to tell her information, and she never did so intentionally. People apparently just found her to have an attentive ear for venting.

"Well, I was told a lot of this gossip when your father was in the hospital getting treatments. But I have also remained friends with a lot of those women, and they are definitely open books. But, I will admit, I have asked in the past why they don't date any of the doctors when they complain about how difficult it is to date. And then they explained that they are legally not allowed to, which makes me think they've had a problem with it in the past, and that's why they've made that rule. But who knows, I'm just speculating at this point. Clearly those nurses need to figure it out though, dipshits," she said as she rolled her eyes and tried to hide her smile.

I laughed in response, causing her to laugh as well. It was funny to hear my mom curse because she had never been one to do so. "Well, you truly never fail to get all the information, warranted or not." I paused. "So you believe me?"

She nodded, getting serious again. "Of course I do, Olivia. I will always believe you. Let me ask my friends what rumors are going around about staff members sleeping together both off and on premise, which is another issue in and of itself. It will be interesting to hear what she says about it."

"Thank you, momma. I appreciate that so much," I said as tears filled my eyes. "I have missed you so much. It feels good to connect like this. Can we make sure we do this at least weekly?"

Before she could respond, she burst into tears on the other end of the video. "Oh honey, whatever you want and need. This gives me comfort, too, knowing I can be there for you in at least some of the ways you need."

I nodded in agreement, in tears after watching my mom. We said our I love yous and goodbyes and hung up. I wiped away my tears, put the journal away then got up to go into the kitchen.

We'd been on the phone for a long time, so I checked my phone for messages from Brent. There was a ten-minute-old message from Brent saying he was on his way, but I didn't know how far he had to drive. To pass the time, I grabbed a snack from the kitchen and sat outside on the bench on the front porch. About ten minutes later, I saw a familiar car turn up the drive

I realized I must have looked like a mess with my IV stand next to me as I ate a snack and enjoyed the newly fallen snow. I breathed in the crisp air and imagined how odd I must look to someone who didn't know the whole story.

He pulled all the way up and parked out of the way of the garages. He stepped out of the car, and I could hear the locking mechanism engage as he came around to the passenger side. He had his hair done and was wearing a heated vest over a long-sleeve henley along with black jeans and a pair of boots to trudge through the snow.

"You look nice, got a hot date after this?" I asked. Albeit flirtatiously, I simply meant to tease him.

"Nope, she's right here," he replied with a wink.

I could feel my heart leap into my throat as I realized he was reciprocating my tone. And even though I meant only to tease him, I could feel a flutter as I realized the door I had potentially opened.

He must have seen the panic on my face as he reassured me. "'Twas a joke my darling. I know you were just teasing. But seriously, no I don't have a date. I just felt like I hadn't gotten ready like this in far too long and wanted to make myself look nice," he said as he shrugged. "Would you like to go inside? Or what's the plan? Your bidding is my command." This time the sarcasm was apparent as he bowed with his arm across his waist.

We busted out laughing as the tension eased from both of us. "I was thinking we could go to one of the ramadas? They're heated and give us some privacy and we get to enjoy the weather," I replied.

"Sounds good to me. Let me help with your stand," he responded, grabbing the stand before I got a chance to accept or decline. He followed closely behind as I led him to one of the ramadas and got comfortable in a snug corner of one of the couches. He adjusted the IV stand to be behind me and the couch but close enough to not create any tugging on the IV site.

"Okay if I sit here?" He asked, gesturing towards the same couch but the opposite corner from me. I nodded, and he took his seat and got comfortable. I grabbed the remote on the side of the couch and turned on the heat along with the firepit that was in the middle.

"So, how have you been?" I asked, not wanting to start into the health conversation just yet.

"I've been okay, just worried about you. I'm sorry you haven't been feeling well," he commented, looking seriously concerned for my health. "I wish I could have done something to help you. But I'm here now for whatever you need."

I took a deep breath as I tried to clear my mind of the anxiety I had. I steeled myself, opened my mouth, and explained everything I thought he deserved to know. I explained my father, his diagnosis, and his death. I talked about the minor health issues I had had, and how they had escalated over the last few months. I talked about Will and what had happened to him. I spilled my guts out to him, unable to stop myself from doing so because of my momentum and the comfort he brought me.

"Wait, that was your brother? I saw a news story on that, but I had never looked into it further. I'm so sorry." I could almost see a glimmer of a tear in his eyes, but I couldn't tell from how far I was sitting from him.

"Yeah, it's been a really difficult time, and some days I just don't know what to do with myself," I said, pausing to try to catch my breath. "I know I'm stressing my mom out even more with my own health. I feel so guilty, I know I don't have control over that, but I just feel horrible. I just want to be better so she doesn't have to worry about me. At one point, I even felt that being dead would be better for her." Trembles coursed through my body as I continued to explain myself. "I know that's crazy, but I just felt that it would be one less thing for her to worry over. But I know she would be devastated. What is wrong with me?!" I was screaming and bawling at this point.

My whaling was deafening as the trembling became uncontrollable, an anxiety attack quickly encroaching on me.

Without hesitation, Brent got up from his corner and rushed to me, embracing me in his arms. I felt his warmth travel through my entire body as I heard his heartbeat against his chest. The melodic rhythm synced with my breathing as I calmed down, and we sat in silence for some time. We stayed embraced as the snow came down, and the little pitter patter as the snowflakes hit the ground.

I closed my eyes, awash with serenity as my stress melted away. I felt Brent shift, pulling me even closer. His embrace made me feel a comfort I hadn't felt in a long time, and I wasn't in any rush to let him go.

Ch 32

After a few minutes, I pulled away and took a deep breath. Brent shifted from holding me close to him to having one hand behind me on the back of the couch while the other rested on my lap. I watched as his eyes went to his hand in my lap and he slowly reached his pointer finger to trace my palm. We both looked up at each other, and I could feel my body tense as a singular bead of sweat dripped down the back of my neck.

What is happening right now?

His green eyes pulled me deeper. My breath shallowed as his hand on the back of the couch brushed my hair behind my ear. The tension was palpable, and I wasn't sure how to handle it. I turned my head to look over the back of the couch at the snowfall to distract myself. I knew I needed to calm myself because I wasn't sure I was ready for anything to happen. I had just told Nathan I needed to focus on myself, and the last thing I wanted to be was a hypocrite and hurt him further.

Brent thankfully read my body language as he slid himself back on the couch a bit to give me more space. While I was thankful, I was also torn. I knew that this was the right direction for things to go, at least in this moment, but it still pained me knowing that I was potentially hurting his feelings. I felt myself disassociating so that I couldn't overthink what all had just happened, but I was quickly snapped back to reality when Brent spoke.

"Would you like to talk more about everything? We don't have to, but I also don't want to close that door for you. Whatever you need, I'm your guy," he said with a genuine smile.

I felt incredibly lucky that I had him in my corner, and though it was filled with a tension beyond friendship, he was putting that aside in order to take care of my needs. It reminded me of every time my mom said that if someone wanted to, they would. If someone wanted to be there for you, they would. If someone wanted to try for you, they would. If someone wanted to love you with every ounce of their being like my father had loved her before he died, they would. I was so grateful to have that example in my life, and I felt like I was witnessing the reality of my mother words at this moment.

"Actually, I'd really like that. But after, can we talk more about you? I know you divulged a lot on the plane, but I'd love to talk about it in more depth and be there for you the same way you are being here for me," I responded, ready to connect with him on an even deeper level.

He smiled as he made eye contact with me and said, "Absolutely, that's an easy enough request. Why don't we start with how you're feeling or have been feeling about the situation with Will. Do you think he has a good chance of coming out of the coma?"

My eyes widened as I realized I hadn't told him about Will squeezing my hand.

"What?" he responded, panic coming through in his tone.

"I forgot to tell you something about all that's happened with him. I was in his room one day, and when I was talking to him, he squeezed my hand. And not like an involuntary twitch that they say you can have in a coma. This was a straight-up hand squeeze in response to something I had said. And then the doctors lied about it and didn't chart it. I'm pretty sure they purposefully omitted it from the paperwork, if I'm being honest. I just can't understand why they didn't take it seriously. Not only that, but the doctor argued with me tooth and nail that I was wrong and that I just felt a spasm," I told him. "I didn't back down. I told my mom when they tried to lie to her. It just doesn't make sense why they would lie like that. What's the point? What does it gain them?"

"That's very odd. I don't see any logic in that either," he replied, his tone sounding confused. "Maybe there's a billing reason? Or maybe the doctor was just being lazy? Either way, it's so messed up to lie about it to your mom. Seems like malpractice to me. You should talk to my dad about it. He's knowledgeable enough to give you advice and refer you out if he thinks you have a good case. Just food for thought," Brent said as he shrugged, not knowing that I had planned on talking to an attorney to evaluate our options. It was one of the things my mom and I had discussed while on Facetime, and I told her I would take care of setting things up so she could focus on Will and working without the stress of trying to research and schedule things.

"That would actually be wonderful," I said. "We were planning on consulting some attorneys to see if we even had a case

237

before we tried proceeding with it."

"Cool, I'll make sure to send you all of his information so you can reach out and talk to him. I'll also let him know who you are to make sure he puts this at the top of his priorities."

"Thank you for doing this for me. You really don't have to, but I appreciate it nonetheless," I replied, feeling some relief.

"Of course. Like I said, we're friends now and my dad has made it clear he's already a fan of yours," he smiled as he made eye contact again.

I could feel the color rise into my cheeks as I tried to turn away as much as I could without being obvious. He looked out the ramada as well, mimicking my positioning.

"So," he said, "was this hospital visit just an ongoing issue of what happened to your head?"

"Uhhh…" I hesitated, looking back at him again. "Not exactly."

"What do you mean not exactly?" he asked, to which I became unsure of what exactly I wanted to say in response. I decided I would tell him the truth, even if it meant opening a completely different door of emotions.

"A girl from my school shoved me backwards, and I tripped and fell and ended up hitting the curb. My medical condition worsened my body's response to it. But yeah, it's been a shit show," I swore, not bothering to catch myself.

"Why did she shove you? What in the hell is all this crap that keeps happening to you?" he asked, genuine concern engulfing his face.

Unable to stop them, I felt tears fill my eyes as I pondered my response to him. I knew I wouldn't be able to lie because my physiological response was far too emotional to do so. I took a deep breath, and as I exhaled, I shakily explained. "She's been a bully since elementary school. That night, she took it a step too far by talking about Will, so I called her out. Clearly, she didn't like that," I finished, laughing through my sobs. Instead of waiting for him to make a comforting move, I decided I needed to lay my head down. I immediately brought it down to Brent's lap, to which he responded by immediately adjusting to make sure I was comfortable in whatever position I ended up laying in. I continued trying to take deep breaths to get through my panicked sobs. All the while, Brent rubbed my head and hair in a soothing manner.

He took the end of his sleeve and gently wiped the tears from my face. I was grateful, not only because he was being sweet, but because my face was freezing from the tears that had stained my cheeks. He then started to rub my back gently, helping me reduce my panicked spasms. And even though my head was killing me in these moments, I knew I had needed to get all of these emotions out, no matter how difficult. And thankfully, Brent had made it a very safe environment for me to do so, and I couldn't thank him enough for that.

Once I had fully calmed down, I explained everything that

had happened with Hannah since elementary school. I shared all of the horrible things she had said about me and my friends, particularly Emma, and how she made life a living hell for anyone that wasn't in her inner circle. I had never understood why she acted like that, but I just assumed she had a garbage home life and couldn't accept herself as-is and felt the need to take it out on others. Whatever the reason, I was glad to tell someone from the outside about it.

He had his hand on my arm and squeezed in a non-verbal "I'm here for you,", then started rubbing my arm shortly after. I took my arm closest to the couch and wrapped it around the front of my body as I set my hand on top of his. His hand was freezing cold, so kept mine on top of his to help it warm up in return for the calm he brought me. He paused for a moment, then continued rubbing my arm as I turned to look up at him. Even though I could only see the underside of his chin, I could still see the definition of his jawline. I didn't get to admire for long as he looked down at me, cocking his head as he did.

"Whatcha lookin at?" he asked.

Goosebumps spread across my arms, and I could feel my face start to tingle, but I couldn't tell if it was from the cold or him looking down at me the way he was. He reached his hand towards my face, brushing my bangs away from my eyes.

I felt a lump start to form, but I quickly cleared it before responding, "I don't think I've ever seen the underside of someone's jaw before. It's just an interesting and new perspective." I took my finger and poked his nose, overestimating how far he was from me.

"Ouch!" he exclaimed as he jerked backwards. "Not cool, Olivia! You'll pay for that!" He started laughing as he moved his hands towards my ribs and started to tickle me. I immediately started to spasm as he tickled my sides incessantly.

"I'm sorry, I'm sorry! I didn't mean it! Apparently my depth perception is worse than I thought," I said through giggles and squirms. He stopped tickling me, but as he did, something didn't quite feel right. I could feel my face flush as I looked up at him and panic set in his eyes.

"Olivia? Olivia? Are you okay?" He asked frantically.

I nodded, ever so slightly, and just held his right hand across my body in my left hand as I tried to regain the blood to my head. The back of my head and neck started to feel moist, so I shot up, which just made my condition worse. What felt like the rest of the blood in my head leaving caused excruciating pain as my stent continued to drain. I squeezed each side of my head in between the palms of my hands to alleviate some of the pressure.

"Can I do anything? Do you need a doctor or nurse? What can I do, please? Please Olivia." Brent was tearing up now, and I could tell that this episode was triggering him. I managed to slowly slide and spin myself around so I was facing him and decided to lean my head forward into his chest. He responded by putting his legs on either side of me as he pulled me into him, rubbing my back at the same time. He then grabbed my hands from my head and started to massage my temples. Immediately, I started to feel relief as I slowly melted against him.

241

I must have drifted off because the next thing I remembered was looking into Brent's eyes as he had his hand under my chin, tipping it upward.

"You okay? I think you may have passed out a bit. Do we need to grab medical personnel?" I responded by shaking my head no. "I'm okay, I promise," I said, smiling ever so slightly. Even though this was a scary episode, the doctor said this type of episode would be normal as I recovered from surgery, but to keep note of anything out of the norm.

Brent had let go of my chin, so I put my arms around his neck as I rested my head against him again. It was a comfort to be able to lean on Brent like this, quite literally and figuratively in this moment. He responded by wrapping his arms around my waist and just letting me sit, yet again, in silence as I focused on willing the pain to go away.

It slowly started to subside as I leaned, and Brent helped by gently rubbing my back. And even though I was improving, I still felt like hot garbage and knew that I needed to get some rest.

"I think you should go inside and lay down," Brent said, as if reading my mind.

"Yeah, that sounds like a great idea," I said as I pulled away and steadied myself on the back of the couch in order to stand up. Before I knew it, Brent was standing next to me, holding me up to make sure I didn't fall.

"I can carry you if you'd like? I can only imagine how

unsteady you feel right now," he said with concern saturating his voice.

I shook my head no, asking him to just help me get to the house. But as soon as I took two steps forward, I knew I wasn't going to make it to the house. Begrudgingly, I turned towards him to ask for help.

"Are you sure you're up for it? The nursing staff can always bring me a wheelchair?"

"I'm certain," he said, swiftly and effortlessly sweeping me off my feet, my arms settling around his neck. He somehow managed to grab my IV stand in the same motion, and we headed back to the house, snow gently dropping around us as we did. I smiled as I looked around at the white flakes surrounding us, taking in the beauty of the winter. And even though I was still in pain, I felt safe.

We got to the front door and Brent set me down, allowing me time to extend my legs before I fully let go. I opened the door, and he continued to help me by spotting me and grabbing my IV stand. We made it back to my room where I immediately got myself into bed and under the covers. I hadn't realized just how cold I had been until I got under the warmth of the blankets, desperately needing to thaw out. As soon as I pulled the top comforter over me, I shivered fairly violently, scaring even myself.

"You okay?" Brent asked, unsure of what to do next.

"Yeah, I'm totally fine. Just didn't realize how cold I was until I got in here," I said, shivering again. "Thank you, I really appreciate you talking to me and helping me get back here. It means a lot."

He smiled affectionately, looking at me as I adjusted my pillow. "Of course, I'm sorry we didn't get to talk more about me. I promise next time will be all about me, and I'll talk about myself so much you'll get sick of me," he said, a huge grin spreading across his face.

"Sounds like a plan to me," I said, reciprocating a smile.

Brent walked up to me, brushing my hair away from my face as he did. He moved his hand down my face, cupping my jaw as his thumb ran across the bottom of my eye to collect remnants of tears I had from my episodes. While he was grabbing my jawline, he pulled my slightly closer as he leaned in and kissed me on the forehead. It was definitely longer than what would be considered friendly, but it wasn't too long to make me uncomfortable.

He pulled away, both his head and his hand, and turned to walk towards the doorway. When he was just a foot away, he turned around to look at me. "Bye, Olivia. Let me know when you want to see me next. I'm open to whatever," he said then quickly turned around and walked out.

I was left alone with my thoughts, but not for long as I felt my phone start to buzz and looked down to see who it was. For whatever reason, guilt immediately engulfed my body as I flipped my phone to see who was calling, even though I had nothing to be guilty for. It was just a spam call that was across my screen, so I ignored it, setting my phone on the nightstand.

I decided laying down for a nap would be my best bet at this point, so I laid myself down, surrounded by pillows and covered in blankets. I fell asleep quickly, able to give my body the break it needed. When I awoke, only an hour had passed, even though it had felt like multiple.

I sat up in the bed, wondering if anyone was home. I grabbed my phone, and sure enough, there was a message from Emma:

Let me know when you're up. I thought we could maybe have a movie night if you're up for it. I got your favorite snacks and drinks.

A smile stretched across my face as I thought about her proposition. *I would love that, I'm ready when you are,* I responded, ending with a kissy face in response to her wink.

Before Emma was able to make it to my room, the nurse came in to check on me. "Are you okay if I give you your meds?" she asked, making me realize that my head was still pounding.

"That would be great," I replied. "Is it of concern if I feel like I'm having a migraine? I know the surgeon said it would be normal, but I just want to make sure that it's not anything I should report to him."

"How about I check your head and dressings while you tell me about your pain so we can just be extra safe about it? How does that sound?" She was genuine in her questions, wanting to make sure I would actually be okay.

I nodded in response, turning my body to face the wall opposite of her so she would have easier access to my incision points and dressings on my head. I told her about my activity that day and that I had had a few emotional episodes when I was with Brent. All the while, she was diligently removing the tape and gauze from my head. I felt a warmth travel down my back as she got the last piece of gauze off from my head.

"Olivia, I am so sorry, but your stent is still draining. I will be right back," she said as she ran out of the room to grab extra supplies. She was back in an instant and cleaning up my neck and back, along with doing her best to get the drainage out of my shirt from the spots where it had managed to get.

"Oh! It's totally okay. Don't worry about the shirt. I am sure the Grandly's will take care of it. They're always happy to help," I said smiling, trying to reassure her that it wasn't a big issue.

She sighed, frustrated at herself. "I'm still so sorry. I hate when a patient's clothes get dirty or ruined. I know it's not the end of the world, but I pride myself in doing what I can to prevent as much as I can, clothing stains included." She stepped back after her careful fussing. "Good news is, all looks good with your incisions, and it looks like your head hurting was from the dressings being a little too tight to allow the best drainage. I will be sure to not stick it down so tightly so it can drain properly and hopefully avoid giving you more migraines. Does your head feel any better?"

"I'm definitely feeling at least some relief. Unfortunately, that means I'm noticing the incision sites now," I said, laughing at myself. "Oh well, better than something being wrong, that's for certain!"

"Very true!" she said in response, a little giggle ending her response.

As she continued to clean, I decided to strike up a conversation with her. "So how long have you been a nurse for? And do you only take care of people in-home, or do you work in a facility too?"

"I've been a nurse for 6 years. I used to work in the hospital in the emergency room, but there was too much drama and the corporate side was just unbearable. I wanted to get into the private sector because people tend to be more grateful, and companies are able to better care for the employees. But I will say, I hope to one day create my own company that will treat nurses with the respect they deserve while giving the best possible care to patients." She stopped bandaging momentarily, then continued back to whatever she was doing. "Thank you for asking, it's nice to know that people care to learn more about me the way I want to learn about them."

"Of course, and I'm glad you feel that way. It's always hit or miss in the hospital when you talk to the nurses and doctors because some of them feel like they couldn't care less and that they're just collecting a paycheck, while others are like you and very caring and clearly passionate about what they're doing. I can only assume that those are the type of nurses you are referencing?" I questioned, knowing I likely hit the nail on the head.

"Bingo!" she exclaimed. "Sorry, a little overzealous for this late in the day, huh?" She giggled at herself this time as she grabbed new gauze to put over my incision. "I just want those people to feel valued, you know? Nursing can be a very unforgiving and underappreciated job, and even if they don't get the gratitude from patients, I would always make sure they got it from me."

"I definitely can see that. I always try to be appreciative, especially since nurses work around the clock to care for patients. The only time I won't is if they're treating me poorly, and even then, I just ask if they're okay. Then, if they want nothing to do with me, I request a switch of nurses. I've only ever asked for one nurse to never be allowed to treat me again, and that was a pretty extreme case." I paused, letting her take in everything I had just said. As the nurse finished my dressings, Emma walked into the room and quietly sat in one of the chairs. Emma was followed in by another nurse, rolling in a cart with my medications and a new IV bag.

When the nurse had completely finished applying all of my dressings and making sure she had cleaned off as much as possible, I turned around and gave her a hug, not knowing what came over me.

She gladly hugged me back, and after I let go and sat back, I wanted to make sure she knew how grateful I was for her. "I just want you to know, you are easily one of the best nurses I've had, and I do truly appreciate you for all that you do for me on a daily basis," I said, sharing a genuine smile.

She sandwiched my hands in between hers, tears welling in her eyes. "Thank you, Olivia. Know that your words mean far more to me than you'll ever know. Now, enjoy your night with your friend. I will be here for a couple more hours, and then I'll be on a new assignment starting tomorrow. We have a newer nurse coming because she needs some extra experience, but she will be here with one of our veterans, so you'll be in great hands. I wish you the best in life, sweetheart. Don't ever lose that fighting spirit of yours." And with that, she left the room and allowed me and Emma to have our own time together.

A minute later, the second nurse finished putting in all of my medications through my IV, hung up my new bag, and asked if I needed anything else. I shook my head and thanked her as she gathered all of the supplies and trash and rolled the cart back out of the room.

Emma hopped up from her chair and came towards the bed. "Hi bestie! How are you feeling? Are you still feeling up for our movie night?."

I nodded, sliding over on the bed so she could take her spot next to me. "What are you in the mood to watch?" I asked, unsure if she already had a movie in mind.

"Honestly, I was thinking some cheesy rom-coms or cartoons? What do you think?" she asked in response.

I thought about it for a minute, but after some thought, I figured that maybe watching some romantic comedies would help bring me some clarity on what to do with Brent and Nathan. We started with *The Notebook*, which ended in both of us bawling our eyes out. And if *The Notebook* made me feel anything, it was that Brent may be the better choice between him and Nathan. Brent reminded me of Noah in his honesty and conviction, even after such a short time of knowing one another. I pushed the thoughts out of my head, though, as we turned on the next movie. We started the first *Bring it On* and I faded out to the sound of squad cheers.

I woke up to Emma being gone and a text explaining that she went to her room so I could sleep. I felt guilty that I had fallen asleep, but Emma was ever-understanding. There was another message notification, which I ignored in order to go back to sleep. I woke up again, this time around 3AM, craving something to drink. While I was well-hydrated from my IV, I still felt parched and decided to go to the kitchen to grab myself something.

I grabbed my IV stand and headed out to the kitchen, noticing a room down the hall for the first time labeled with "medical personnel" for the nurses and doctors to stay in overnight. I continued my venture down to the kitchen and turned on the lights under the cabinets to minimize the brightness. I grabbed a banana and some blueberries from the fridge and sat down to eat them. After I was done with my blueberries, I noticed a basket of goodies sitting on the counter by the door and some flowers in a vase next to them. I lifted myself from the chair to take a look.

The goodies consisted of some snacks and a little blue bear and some other sweet sentiments. I tried to refrain from touching it as I didn't know whose it was, but I was curious if it was for me, and if it was, who it was from. As I went to smell one of the flowers, I jumped, startled by a voice behind me. I turned around to see a figure in the doorway.

"Oh, I'm so sorry Olivia. Didn't mean to sneak up on you like that," the figure said, emerging from the shadow of the door frame. It was the overnight nurse, and I wondered if she just happened to be coming to the kitchen as well, or if she heard me coming down the hall. "Those are both for you. The flowers are from your mom, but the basket didn't have a name on it when it arrived. There is a little note in it though if you want to take a look," she explained.

I turned back to the basket and found the note she referenced. I pulled it out of its envelope and flipped it rightside-up to read.

I know that time has not been on our side, but I know I'm ready for a ride.

While I immediately thought it was from Brent, I couldn't shake the feeling that the message was more cryptic. I flipped over the card to see another message:

P.S. Know that I am always near, whether you need me least or are in fear.

I felt a shiver travel down my spine as the feeling in my gut started to grow.

"Did it say who sent those to you?" the nurse asked.

I turned around, forcing a smile on my face as I responded, "No, but I have a good feeling I know who it's from." I tried to shake the assumptions my brain was making as I slid the card back into the envelope and set it back in the basket.

"That's great! It was very sweet of whomever sent that over to you. Would you like some help to take it back to the room?"

I immediately nodded my head yes, having learned my lesson from the multiple times I had refused others' help over the past couple of weeks, and months, even. I grabbed my banana in one hand and my IV stand in the other and started heading back to my room. The nurse was right behind me, able to carry the basket in one hand and the flowers in her other.

Once we made it back to the room, I sat myself on the bed, getting situated to bring my legs back up as exhaustion swept over me once more. The nurse must have been able to tell I was struggling as she set down the stuff and immediately came over to the side of the bed to help me. We got my right leg up, my left leg quickly following as I tucked myself under the covers.

"Thank you for helping me. I realize I haven't formally met you yet," I said, reaching my hand out to shake hers.

She reached her hand to meet mine, and grabbed, giving me a tight but comfortable handshake. "I'm Natalie. It's very nice to meet you, Olivia. How are you feeling? I have meds that I'm able to give you right about now if you'd like them."

"That would be great, actually. I think my brain and body both need to chill out."

She agreed and ran out of the room to grab the cart. She was back in moments, medications all lined up for my needs. She quickly added all of the inflammation and preventative medications along with some anti-nausea since that was my most consistent symptom.

"On a scale of one to ten, how much pain are you in right now?" she asked, pain medication vial in hand.

"This has been one of my better nights, so I'm around a 6 right now. I think I would be good with half a normal dose to be honest," I said, wanting to reduce how much of the narcotics were going through my bloodstream.

"You read my mind. That's exactly what I was hoping to do. I have no problem if you need the full dosage, though. I just hate giving more if a patient doesn't feel like they need it," nurse Natalie responded, preparing the syringe with the pain medication. She acquired half the normal amount and slowly put it into my IV. Because it wasn't as much as normal, it didn't make me feel super groggy and out of it, so I thought I would try to strike up a conversation.

"So how long have you been a nurse?" I asked.

"I've been one for 12 years, believe it or not. I graduated high school at 16 and managed to get into a dual BA/nursing program. So I was able to get my degree and certification in half the time because of credits I had taken in high school." She paused, a look of concern crossing her face. "I'm so sorry, I didn't mean for that to come across braggy or anything. I guess I didn't think through what I was saying as I was saying it."

As someone who was avid about school, it was humbling to hear about the success of the intelligent woman before me. "Please, don't apologize," I said. "You busted your ass to get to where you are, you have every right to be proud of that. No one should tell you otherwise."

She smiled bashfully as she detached the syringe from my IV. "Thank you for that. It's very sweet of you to say. I often get so lost in talking about my education that sometimes people take offense to what I'm saying."

I thought about that for a minute before replying. "Sounds like those people are just jealous that they aren't as successful as you have been," I said, shrugging my shoulders. "Also, if you need to get back to bed, you are more than welcome to go because I completely understand. But if you're up for it, I wouldn't mind if you pulled up a chair to chat," I said, smiling at her.

"I'm actually wide awake, so I'd love to chat with you," Natalie said as she smiled back at me. She grabbed a lounger and pulled it closer to the bed. "With that said, I have a question for you. How are you feeling? And not just in this moment, but overall? I know you have been through some rough times lately, and you are more than welcome to talk to me about them if you'd like."

I looked at her, feeling relieved. A wave of emotions came over me. As this wave was hitting, I felt tears start to stream down my face uncontrollably. Natalie sat forward in her chair as she grabbed my hand in hers, squeezing it to give me comfort.

After a few minutes, I calmed down and was able to tell her about the events of my life, starting with my dad's diagnosis. I told her about his illness, the struggles that my family had with his sharp decline, my depression and anxiety, my mom struggling with things—everything. I explained how I always put on a front so my mom would focus on Will, and how she had felt like a failure for not being able to parent to her own expectations. I told her about how I knew that I would need to be strong for my family by helping around the house, helping Will both emotionally and with school, and just making sure that everything was taken care of to the best of my abilities.

Then I told her about Nathan and how our relationship blossomed, and then about Will and the fire—how he was in the hospital and would potentially never wake up. That's when I lost it again. I missed him; I missed talking to him; I missed giving him hugs; I missed how every morning before we went to school, we would tease each other then compliment one another so that we would leave the house on a positive note. I missed helping him with homework, and I even missed when he would get frustrated and throw a book across the room because he wasn't understanding the material, only to feel silly a few minutes later when I was able to explain the concept in a different way. But I missed the fact that he reminded me of my father and gave my mom comfort the most.

I calmed down once again and continued by telling her how things had gone since the fire. I told her about how my health quickly declined after Will was admitted, and how we found out that I had a blood disorder. I told her everything up to the day before, when I had my movie night with Emma, and how I was so grateful for her friendship and the care from the Grandly's.

I took a deep breath and locked eyes with Natalie as I did. "I'm so sorry, I know that was a lot. I just have felt so lost in my thoughts lately, it was nice to spill some of my guts about it."

She smiled at me, responding, "That's why I asked. As someone in the medical profession, I see a lot of people struggling with not only the day-to-day, but the big picture, too. And that often gets lost in all of the stresses of the day-to-day, to the point where people can fall apart mentally and are never able to really fully recover from whatever is going on. I hoped you would be able to vent to me, so no apologies necessary. Let's focus on something that is clearly bothering you right now that maybe I can help with. What do you plan to do about the boys?"

I had been pushing the intrusive thoughts about them from my mind, and I knew I needed to figure things out for the sake of my tearing heart. "I honestly don't know what to do. I don't even know what to think. I feel like Nathan wasn't lying when he made all those promises. And I also feel like it's very much not like him to act like this."

"Well, let's think it through. What changed? Anything major?" she asked.

"I mean, I told him that I needed time to focus on myself. And that I wasn't ready for anything with him just yet. I figured that would be okay since he promised he would wait for me. He told me what I needed was a priority, and that his needs would always come second through all of this. Not that I fully agreed with that, but I at least hoped that he would follow with the first part," I said, lowering my head. "I just can't wrap my head around why Nathan would suddenly vanish from my life as quickly as he came, you know? Like, for what? What did lying to me gain for him? His parents are friends with my mom, too, so it just adds to my confusion."

"Oh, I totally get it. Sometimes boys say things they don't mean, both in a positive and negative way. And when they're upset, they definitely say things they don't mean. Is there anything that maybe happened at home or in his personal life that you know of? Maybe school? Or his family?" she asked.

Obviously, his arrest. I had omitted that information from our conversation because I didn't want to talk about a story that wasn't mine.

"I honestly don't know. I wish I did though. I doubt it was his family because he has a great relationship with them. There was an incident that I was worried about…" I trailed off, the blood rushing from my face.

"Olivia, are you feeling okay? You just went extremely pale."

Natalie got up from her chair to hold onto my shoulder.

"Ye-ye-yes. I'm fine," I stuttered. "I need Emma, please, it's urgent. I know it's early morning, but she will understand. Can you grab her for me please?" The desperation in my voice became palpable as a million thoughts raced through my head.

"Yes, of course. As long as you're sure you're okay?" Natalie's worry had spread across her face, particularly highlighting the concern in her eyes.

"Yes, I promise. I just need to talk to her about something. I'm sorry, I wish I could talk to you about it. I just don't want to divulge someone else's story to someone I don't know personally. I hope you understand," I said, looking up at Natalie.

"Oh, hun, you don't have to worry about my feelings. You can say as little or as much as you would like to me. I will never fault you for not wanting to talk to me about something. I totally get it. Let me go grab Emma for you."

"Thank you," I said, and with that, she left.

Ch 34

My diaphragm tightened as the sound of erratic palpitations filled my ears, deafening me as I watched Natalie leave the room. I realized what had happened with Nathan, and I needed to talk to Emma about it. I couldn't believe I hadn't seen it before, and that I had completely neglected his court case as of late. My epiphany was overwhelming, but seemed to make more and more sense as I thought about it further.

Natalie came back into the room shortly after leaving. "I'm so sorry, Olivia. But it looks like Emma isn't home."

I grabbed my phone to see what time it was, and it was already 6AM. Emma was likely out doing photography to build her portfolio. I checked to see if I had any texts from her, but there was only a message from Brent saying *Good Morning*. I left it unread, as I wasn't ready to talk to anyone but Emma. I shot her a quick message asking where she was and what her plan was for the day before turning back to Natalie, who was standing in the doorway.

"That's okay. I appreciate you running over there for me. I just sent her a message, so hopefully she'll let me know what her schedule looks like." I paused, hesitating to ask her more questions.

My face must have given me away because Natalie responded by saying, "you can ask whatever just came across your mind. I really don't mind at all."

"I—I just had some more questions about your experience and workplaces. Have you ever worked for the local hospital?" I asked, unsure if she was going to actually answer any of the questions that came to mind.

"I did, but I didn't last long due to the culture. Why do you ask?" Natalie responded, taking a seat back in the chair she had been in earlier.

"I have concerns about the treatment of both myself and my brother. And I was wondering, do they get a lot of reports against them?"

She hesitated, shifting in the chair and visibly uncomfortable.

"You don't have to answer that; please don't feel pressured to do so," I said frantically in hopes that she would only do what she was comfortable doing.

"No, no, I don't mind," Natalie replied, her hesitation still apparent. "I will say, they have a lot of issues that are hidden from the public. It's a huge reason why I left. I didn't want to risk my licensing and reputation based on the hospital's issues. I also pride myself in the care of my patients, and they seem to care more about monetary gain than anything. But please don't let anyone know that unless you're talking to a lawyer. It can get you into a lot of trouble because that hospital goes to great lengths to hide things and suppress both patients and employees. I would know."

"Can I ask about a particular issue to know if there's a pattern? I plan on talking to an attorney on behalf of my mom, and I just want to make sure there is something established and not that I'm just losing my mind," I said, realizing our case may be much stronger than I originally anticipated.

"Of course. I can't promise I will be able to answer, but I will do my best," Natalie said.

"Do doctors or nurses have any issues with things not getting charted? Whether on purpose by neglecting to document them or by accident because it was forgotten?" I asked, crossing my fingers that she would be able to answer.

"Yes. I can't go into more details than that, but absolutely, yes. They are notorious for that issue. Is that what you think happened with you or Will?"

"No, I *know* it happened. I witnessed a doctor tell my mom that Will had no progress and when I called them out, the original doctor denied anything even happened. Will had grabbed my hand in response to me talking to him, and they didn't notate it, and when confronted, they claimed it was just a typical twitch within a coma. I had felt those twitches before, but this movement was nothing like them. This seemed purposeful—not a normal occurrence for his condition," I explained. I hoped to gain an ally for the impending journey my mom and I would face against the hospital.

"Are you kidding me? They didn't even document it? That is absolutely ridiculous," she said, her knuckles turning white as her fists tightened. I looked at Natalie, taking in this incredible nurse who had been spending all this time with me. Her hair was purposefully tousled, her scrubs crisply ironed, and she appeared overall put together. "Even if they felt it was just an involuntary twitch within the coma, they should have still documented it because that can be an important factor in future diagnoses, prognoses, and even treatment. That is absolutely infuriating. I'm so sorry that happened to you, but I am glad that you spoke up and told your mom. You should be proud of yourself for doing that. So many people stay silent, and it never ends well," she said, locking eyes with me.

I started to tear up thinking about the consequences had I not said anything. "I'm glad I did, too, because they said he had no chance of survival and attempted to take him off of life support. If I hadn't said anything, they would have killed him. Instead, my mom was able to get him transferred to Arizona."

"Wow. Olivia, that's amazing. You speaking up for your brother when he needed you most probably saved his life." She paused. "All of this because some doctors couldn't get it together. You know what? Let me know when you talk to a lawyer. I will be a witness for you if you need it. I am more than happy to put them in their place for their violations against our medical code of honor," Natalie said, reaching her hands out to grab mine again. She cupped my hands between hers before continuing. "You should be so proud of yourself. Not only for standing up for Will, but standing up for yourself and your mom, and for handling all of these struggles with such grace."

"Th—thank you. That means a lot," I said, gasping for air as I felt myself get choked up. She stood up, still grabbing my hand and holding it close to her.

"Let it all out, Olivia. It's not good to hold things in. You have been through a significant amount of trauma in just the last couple months, let alone the last few years. You deserve to show your emotions in a safe environment."

I started to cry, but my cries slowly turned into quiet wails. As I let my emotions show, everything I had been through flashed through my mind like a photo album. Every moment I had struggled with made itself known, and I couldn't help but feel selfish for thinking of myself in a time like this.

With Natalie still holding onto me, I started to do breathing and grounding exercises to calm myself down. As I did this, my phone started to buzz, and Natalie let me go so I could grab my phone from the nightstand. I looked to see who was calling, but it was a number I didn't recognize. For whatever reason, my gut told me to answer, even though I never answered random numbers.

"Hello?" I answered.

"Honey? It's me." The familiar voice on the other end of the phone had given me so much comfort on so many occasions. But this time, nothing but dread overcame me. It was my mom. And she was not calling from her phone, which couldn't mean anything good.

"Mom?" I choked out, knowing she would hear the fear in my voice.

"Baby, I need you to get to Arizona," she said, more serious than I had ever heard her in my life.

"No," I whispered. Barely audible, my "no" signified not that I was unwilling to go, but that I was in utter disbelief of what this meant. "Momma, no, please no. Please don't tell me this is what I think it means."

"I'm so sorry, Olivia. I was hoping things would get better, I really was. But we're trending in the wrong direction, and quickly. I wanted to make sure you got to say your goodbyes because I couldn't live with myself if you didn't. I booked you and your doctor a ticket for this morning at 10. I'll grab you both from the airport and bring you straight here," she said, pausing. Ten seconds of silence seemed like ten years before she said, "I emailed you both of the boarding passes. I'll see you soon, okay? I love you my baby girl. I love you so much, and I'm so sorry. I wish I could change this, I really do."

"Okay, I'll get ready and see you soon," was all I could muster up in response.

"See you soon," she responded, hanging up the phone.

I set the phone back on the nightstand and looked up at Natalie. She remained silent, inferring what I had just learned and giving me the moment that I needed.

I let out a spine chilling wail as I collapsed into a pile onto the bed. Natalie came close enough to rub my back, but not too close to invade my space.

I couldn't believe this. My baby brother? He was going to be gone, too? After losing our dad? And for what? Because someone decided to vandalize a kids' playground? Or was it because someone wanted to hurt my family beyond repair?

Before I could think further about it, Mr. and Mrs. Grandly ran into the room. "What happened?! Are you okay, Olivia? Natalie, what's going on? We heard that all the way from the other side of the wing," Mr. Grandly frantically questioned.

"Hi Mr. Grandly," Natalie responded. "She's okay physically. But I'll let her tell you what happened when she's ready and able." She continued to rub my back as I strained to look at him.

"W-W-Will. He-he is declining. A-a-and quickly," I mustered, stuttering through my words. I took a deep breath, looking at the ceiling as I tried to compose myself. Once I was able to breathe properly, I continued. "My mom bought me a ticket to fly out to Arizona to say my goodbyes. I-I-I'm not ready." Tears filled my eyes again but refused to pour out. I sighed, trying to catch my breath.

"Oh, Olivia, dear girl. What can we do? How can we help? Whatever you need, we will be here and do whatever we can," Mrs. Grandly responded.

"I just need a ride to the airport, please. My mom already got flights for me and the doctor at 10 a.m." I responded.

"You got it," Mr. Grandly said. "I'll grab our driver and make sure you have everything you need ready to go for your flight. How long will you be out there so I know exactly what you need?"

"Just for the night. I will be back tomorrow."

"Okay, I will take care of all of those arrangements. And I will let Emma know, too. She is out in the wilderness and likely doesn't have service. She went with a group for a photography course, so she probably just left the phone in her car, or it's buried in her camera bag as usual. Do you need us to try to find people in the group so we can get a hold of her?" he asked.

"No, absolutely not. While I appreciate the sentiment, I want her to enjoy herself out there. It's the least she deserves for how incredible she is and continues to be," I replied, my eyes slowly starting to close. But before they could fully shut, I could see the tears that started to well in both Mr. And Mrs. Grandly's eyes. "It's okay. I promise it will be okay. Everything happens for a reason. Sometimes it's not a reason we like, but a reason we need."

I felt a squeeze around my hand. No words were needed during that moment. I could hear footsteps leave the room as another pair entered. I forced my eyes open, and there was the doctor with his white coat standing next to the bed. He had medications on a tray ready to go along with a bag of the medications I would potentially need within the next 24 hours, up to a couple days to be safe.

"Olivia," the doctor said. "You can go to sleep. I know you need the rest. I am going to give you your medications once we get on the plane, including your sedative, so that you can rest until we get to Arizona. Does that sound okay to you?"

I nodded, barely able to force the motion. We left for the airport, arriving at a special terminal since our plane was a smaller charter. The doctor wheeled me to the plane after checking us in. He assisted me in getting up the stairs, and once I was settled in, he handled all of the logistics.

Once he sat down next to me, he got me ready to administer the medications. My eyes slowly closed as he injected the sedative. I felt myself drift off, the only thing on my mind being Will.

Ch 35

When I woke up, I was in the hospital in a bed. But this time, I wasn't alone. My mom was in a lounge chair nearby, as was my doctor. Not even two feet to my right, there was Will, still hooked up to every wire, tube, and machine imaginable. He was jaundiced, his skin and nails closer to the color of mustard than to the natural tone of his skin. I reached my right arm out to clutch his hand. Grasping it, I rolled over to my right side so I could face him.

I immediately started to cry again, this time keeping my noise level to a minimum with my silent sobs. This was my baby brother, his lifeless body completely still under mine. I couldn't believe this was happening.

I turned my gaze towards my mom. "What exactly did the doctors say?"

My mom looked at me, grabbing the paperwork next to her. "They said his prognosis is not looking good and that all of his vitals are quickly dropping, which shows that his organs are starting to shut down. All they said beyond that was that we should start making arrangements and say our goodbyes because they don't think he would make it past a couple days, at most. I knew when I heard the news that I needed to get you out here."

"Thank you, mom. I appreciate that. Will I be able to have some alone time with him at some point? I just want to share some things with him in privacy." I was unsure of how my mom would react to this knowing that she likely, and rightfully, wanted to spend as much time with him as possible.

"Absolutely. I will be going to my hotel for the night, so you will have all night with him to chat. I need the rest anyway, and since I've been here every day, it's your time to have with him," she replied.

That was my mother, the least selfish and most humble person I had ever known. "Will you be back in the morning before I leave again so we can all be together as a family for one last time?" I asked, the question breaking off another piece of my soul in the process.

"Yes, honey. Of course," she said as she walked towards me. She hugged me as she kissed my forehead, and I took the moment to hold her in my arms and not let go. I needed her hug just as much as she needed mine, and we were lost in the moment believing that it would bring us some sort of comfort.

She gently let go and started to pull away, my arms loosening their grip around her as she took a step backwards. "I love you, Olivia. I hope you get to say whatever goodbyes you need to."

And with that, she left the room, leaving me alone with just Will and my thoughts. My practitioner had already left the room, I assumed to respect the privacy I wanted with Will.

I sat up in the bed, pressing the buttons so that the back would incline with me, crossing my legs as I did. I grabbed his hand closest to me and set it in my lap, covering it with my own. I leaned over, placing my head on his bed. I could feel tears stream as I wished for a miracle, knowing that it wasn't likely at this point.

A nurse came into the room after a few minutes, and upon seeing me, profusely apologized and insisted she could come back later.

"No, no, it's okay. Do whatever you need for him. I'll stay out of the way."

She walked over to the other side of his bed to take a look at his stats and chart them. She started to walk out of the room when I decided to ask her a question.

"Is Will still on meds? Or have the doctors just pulled out of everything?" I asked, needing to know how hopeless they believed his case to be.

She opened the chart and swiped through the pages. "It looks like they stopped medications on him a few days ago. The notes show the doctor said that he was concerned that they were just making Will worse, so they took him off to not cause additional harm."

"Thank you, I appreciate the honesty. Have a good rest of your shift if you don't find your way back in here."

She nodded and continued her way out of the room. I turned my attention back to Will as I started to tell him about all of the frivolous, stupid things I was dealing with. I wanted to talk to him like things were normal— as though we were back home. After telling him about the "small" things, I started talking to him about all of the good memories that had flashed in my mind over the last few weeks. I told him all of the things I loved about him, and how he was an amazing little brother. And that even though I wouldn't be able to hold him anymore, I was happy that dad would. I knew how much Will missed him, and if there was any chance that Will could hear anything I was saying, I wanted him to leave in comfort, not in fear.

After a while, my doctor came back in to ask how I was feeling and to give me my medications. He gave me my full doses, causing me to immediately drift off.

I woke up hours later to a dark sky. I was incredibly groggy, unable to lift my head. I was still on my right side, facing Will. I was able to muster the energy to grab his hand once more as I started to drift off again.

In my dream state, I could see the light of the door as it opened and closed behind whoever had walked in. It looked like a nurse, and she seemed familiar, but I wasn't able to put a finger on it. She approached the free side of Will's bed, and it looked as though she administered something into Will's IV before hastily leaving out of the door. While I couldn't shake the feeling that something was off, I figured my mind was just playing tricks on me, per the usual.

I woke up the next morning to my mom rubbing my arm, feeling as if I had been hit by a bus and dragged down the road. I sat up, and that's when the wave of nausea hit me. "Mom, I need a puke bucket and pronto," I said, frantically trying to keep my stomach contents down long enough for her to get it to me. Just in the knick of time, she pushed one in front of my face for me to empty some acid and the little bread I had had the night before. While I felt better, my doctor grabbed some of my intravenous nausea medication and put it through, granting me total relief.

"Are you okay?" my mom asked, concern sweeping across her face.

"Yeah, I'm good now. I think I just sat up too quickly," I replied.

"Okay good, I can only handle so much right now," she said, her face paling. "How was last night? Were you able to tell Will everything you wanted to?"

"Yes, but can I ask for something? Can I please stay at least for a couple more days? I know he's not awake, but I get more comfort being next to him than I would just leaving him again, especially knowing what I do now."

My mom looked at me, a smile on her mouth that didn't translate to her eyes. "Of course. I'll change your ticket." She turned to my doctor. "You are more than welcome to go back home if you'd like. Please don't feel obligated to stay, I'm sure she'll get any care she might need here."

"I am absolutely fine with staying, as long as you are okay with it. I have all of her medications and dosages and everything. No need to add additional stress by trying to explain things to another practitioner. I am happy to be here and help," he said, smiling.

My mom's shoulders visibly relaxed as relief fell across her body. "Thank you, that would be wonderful." She started dialing a number as she left the room, presumably calling the airline to switch our flights.

I chatted with my doctor, telling him how I was feeling. He grabbed some supplies to change out the dressing on my head while we chatted, bringing me even more relief than the previous change had. After he was done, my mom walked back into the room and let us know she had switched everything with our flights so that we could stay indefinitely. We spent the rest of the day reminiscing, happy to be spending this time with my family, no matter how somber. The time flew by, and soon my mom was heading back to her hotel again, leaving me to my thoughts.

Ch 36

I stayed awake, unable to fall asleep while thinking about the dream I had the night before. I asked my doctor to let the staff know that I wanted no one to visit at night unless it was to check on Will's stats. I needed to be able to determine dreams from reality. He was happy to oblige, and staff made sure to keep an eye on the room. No one came into the room that night except familiar nurses.

The next few days were a blur, people hustling and bustling in and out of the room, doing nothing but documenting any changes and helping my mom set up palliative care. She decided on cremating him to put him next to my dad so they would be next to one another for as long as she was alive. She set up a service to celebrate his life, scheduling all of the necessary pieces such as venue, food, and flowers.

Deja vu overcame me as I recalled my mother's same actions years ago. We had time to prepare then. We didn't this time, and my heart broke for my mom.

My mom finalized the scheduling and even had a priest come in to bless Will, though we weren't religious. I think it brought her peace to know that she had done everything she could to make his passing as smooth as possible for both us and him.

The last night before going back home was the heaviest for me. I could feel a huge weight on my chest as I tried to breathe and ground myself, unable to stay calm. I was also unable to sleep the night before and unwilling to take sleep aids because I wanted to be awake as much as possible during the remaining time I had with Will.

As hard as I fought to stay awake, I started to fall asleep in the wee hours of the morning around 3, unable to keep my eyes open. As my body drifted, I maintained an alert state of consciousness. All of the events I had been through with Will started flashing before me, almost as if I could reach out and touch them. In the last scene, I was able to see both myself and Will laying down in our beds: me asleep, him looking like he came out of a medical textbook. I could see my body twitching in response to all of the memories I was experiencing, but that wasn't what caught my eye. Will's hand was twitching, something it hadn't done since I arrived a few short days prior.

While I noticed his hand twitch, I could not have predicted what happened next. Will sat up straight in his bed, choking on the tubes coming from his throat as he grunted a barely audible, "Liv?"

I woke up, pouring sweat, shooting up in my bed. I turned to look at my still-lifeless brother, but to my surprise, a figure was next to the bed. "Who are you?!" I exclaimed, the figure quickly running out of the room. Moments later, my doctor came in, his face dripping in concern.

"Olivia? Are you okay?"

Adrenaline still pounding through my body, all I could muster was shaking my head no. I was able to take a few deep breaths before actually being able to respond with words. "Someone. Someone was in here. They were over there, next to Will's bed. I couldn't tell who it was or what they were wearing, but it wasn't a nurse. At least not one that was supposed to be in here because they ran out as quickly as you ran in." My body trembled as I tried to calm myself.

"I'll work with the staff to figure out who it was. Try to calm your breathing so your blood pressure lowers. Last thing you need is something happening to you with your blood pumping as hard as it is right now," the doctor said, leaving the room.

I was able to calm myself, but I was never able to fall back asleep. I stayed up the rest of the night, readying myself for departure in the morning at 9 o'clock.

My mom walked into the room, giving me a hug as soon as she did. "I'm going to miss you honey. But I'll be home as soon as I have everything settled here." She turned and looked at Will. "At least he's looking better," she commented, referring to the jaundice of his skin that had faded. Even though we had accepted him as gone, it was comforting to see him look like his normal self again.

My mom left the room again to have a conversation with the doctors for next steps.

I faced Will, saying what would likely be my last goodbyes, grabbing his left hand in mine. I wiped the tears that fell onto his hand as I apologized to him for feeling like I had failed him. I told him how much I loved him. And I told him I looked forward to the day we would meet again.

As I went to set his hand back down on the bed, I felt his hand twitch. I brushed it off momentarily, turning to grab my water from the table next to my bed. As I did, I felt more movement. I whipped back around. "Will? Will, can you hear me?" Another twitch, almost as if he was trying to communicate.

I turned to face the hospital room door and screamed, "Mom! Mom! Come back in here! I think..." I was unable to finish my sentence, distracted by Will's bed shifting behind me. I swiveled, coming face to face with my little brother.

Will had sat up, locking eyes with me after I turned. And just as he had done in my dream, a choked out "Liv?" left his lips.

www.ingramcontent.com/pod-product-compliance
Lightning Source LLC
Chambersburg PA
CBHW070000200626
46811CB00021B/2562